THE FRIENDS

OTHER YEARLING BOOKS YOU WILL ENJOY:

YEARLING BOOKS are designed especially to entertain and enlighten young people. Patricia Reilly Giff, consultant to this series, received her bachelor's degree from Marymount College and a master's degree in history from St. John's University. She holds a Professional Diploma in Reading and a Doctorate of Humane Letters from Hofstra University. She was a teacher and reading consultant for many years, and is the author of numerous books for young readers.

THE Friends

KAZUMI YUMOTO

TRANSLATED BY CATHY HIRANO

A Yearling Book

Visit us on the Web! www.bdd.com

Educators and librarians, visit the BDD Teacher's
Resource Center at www.bdd.com/teachers

ISBN: 0-440-41446-6

Reprinted by arrangement with Farrar, Straus and Giroux, Inc.

Printed in the United States of America

June 1998

10 9 8 7 6

OPM

PO

THE FRIENDS

1

It has been raining steadily since the beginning of June, and it's raining hard again today. The opening of our school's swimming pool has been put off until tomorrow. I gaze absently out the window at the "monster leaves." Shaped like the palm of a hand and roughly the size of a pumpkin, the huge leaves have already grown as high as the classroom windows on the second floor. Every time it rains they grow taller. In winter they shrivel up and die, yet each spring they come back to life, and by summer they're shooting up everywhere like alien creatures.

It was in second grade that I privately began calling them monster leaves. I was shorter then. Nobody called me Beanpole like they do now, and my front teeth had not yet been replaced by oversized adult teeth. In other words, I was still a cute little kid. I worried about things like whether the school lunch would be so revolting that I wouldn't be able to eat it, and the sixth-graders playing handball seemed really big and strong and somewhat frightening.

That innocent little second-grader, yours truly, was totally absorbed by his discovery of this new creature, the monster leaves. My second-grade classroom was on the first floor, just below the room I'm in now. Every morning when I'd enter, the first thing I'd do was inspect the monster leaves. I was sure that at night, under cover of darkness, they sprouted eyes and mouths like jack-o'-lanterns. When they had grown as high as the second floor, I'd lean out the window and gaze up at them with my heart pounding, certain that something awful would happen. Now I'm sitting in the very same room that I had gazed up at so long ago. And now I am a sixth-grader, though not nearly as strong and scary as I had once imagined sixth-graders to be.

Tired of looking at the leaves, I glance around the room. This is the third day that Yamashita has been absent from school. He even missed the test at cram school on Sunday, which you should never do, so I haven't seen him for four days. He didn't seem to have a cold when I saw him on Saturday, so I wonder what could have happened.

Yamashita's seat is in front of mine one row over. The comic book he left on the shelf in his desk is in plain view. If the teacher finds it, he'll confiscate it. But Yamashita has always been like that. A bit out of it.

4   "Kiyama!"

Oh great. The teacher is calling on me. I stand up as slowly as I can.

"The answer, Kiyama?"

"Um . . ."

"Wrong. Not 'um.' "

Kawabe, who sits behind me, is poking me in the butt. "Round," he whispers.

"Round," I repeat tentatively.

"Yes. And?"

"Smooth," Kawabe prompts.

"Smooth," I repeat.

"Right, round and smooth." The teacher is rubbing the top of his shiny, bald head. "Just like me." He is looking at me expectantly. "And whom do you think we are talking about?"

Kawabe isn't giving me any more hints. I panic. Round and smooth? Round and smooth? Who could it be?

"Buddha!" I blurt out desperately.

The whole classroom erupts with laughter.

"Idiot! Just what class do you think this is?"

"Huh?"

"Round and smooth. The characteristics of pebbles in the earth's stratum. Pay attention!"

I shrink back into my seat with everyone still staring at me, suppressing their giggles. I'd been trapped! It's all Yamashita's fault, I think, reaching out with my foot to move Yamashita's chair so that the comic book doesn't show so much. Kawabe pokes me in the back.

"What do you want?"

"Did you hear why Yamashita is absent?"

"No, why?"

"His grandmother died. His grandmother in the country."

"What?" I didn't even know he had a grandmother. I mean, I know everybody has grandparents, but he's never talked about a grandmother, and I've never heard any mention of "the country."

"He's gone to the funeral. That's what my mom told me."

"Really?"

"You ever been to a funeral?"

"Nope."

"Me neither. When the old man in my apartment building died a while ago, my mom went to the wake, but . . ."

"You mean you actually *want* to go to a funeral?"

"Well, it's not that I really want to, it's just— Ow!"

"Kawabe! Kiyama!" the teacher bellows.

Kawabe straightens his crooked glasses and rubs his forehead. The teacher's chalk was right on target.

"What are you whispering about? Stand at your desks for the rest of the class!"

The next day Yamashita is back at school. I catch sight of him from behind as he goes through the school gate.

"Hey, Pudge!" I call out, and then regret it instantly. Kawabe and I always call him that, not to be mean, but because it seems to be the obvious choice. I mean he *is* pudgy. Every time we call him that, it's like we're saying, "Yeah, you're fat. So what?" He pretends to be mad, but we know he really isn't. But today the face he turns to me seems kind of down. I should have known better. His beady little eyes, which are always blinking, seem dull and bleary. Worse still, he doesn't even look mad at me for calling him Pudge. I feel pretty lousy. After all, he just came back from a funeral.

We walk silently into the school yard. Maybe I should say something comforting. But what?

"Hey, Pudge! I heard your grandma died!"

Kawabe! That idiot! I look up and see him leaning precariously from the second-floor window, yelling at the top of his lungs. As usual, he wasn't thinking. In fact, I don't believe Kawabe has ever had a thought in his life.

Yamashita looks a little embarrassed, but then, to my astonishment, he yells back, "Yup. She sure did!" What can he be thinking? I know that Kawabe never thinks, but Yamashita? After all, she was his own *grandmother*. I can't figure him out at all.

But then how could I understand? I have never been to a funeral. My grandfather died, but that was before I was born, so I have no idea how I would feel.

Then, because Kawabe is leaning too far out the window, his glasses, which are, next to his life, the most important thing he possesses, slip from his face and fall to the ground below. The lenses break with a dull crack. Without his glasses, Kawabe is helpless. He is still fumbling about, looking for the classroom door, when Yamashita and I reach the room. Sugita and Matsushita tease him so unmercifully that he finally bursts into tears.

Kawabe's mother comes and takes him home, and I give up any idea of asking Yamashita about the funeral. I just can't think of how to bring the subject up. Yamashita seems the same as always. In other words, he spent the entire gym period trying to do a flip on the bars and not succeeding, he couldn't read the assignment in language class, and he broke the glass slide for the microscope in the science experiment. But at times he seemed kind of absentminded, as if he was staring at one little speck on the wall. And come to think of it, he didn't have seconds at lunchtime, even though it was fried noodles, his favorite dish.

Every day, Monday to Friday, we have cram school after regular school. We're there from six until eight and sometimes even until nine o'clock at night, trying to cram in everything we'll need to know to pass the entrance exams for junior high school next year. By the time we get out, we're exhausted, not to mention starving. The three of us always buy yogurt drinks and slurp them through straws while we wait in the dark on the bench at the bus stop. I was sure Kawabe would skip cram school today because of his glasses, but he didn't. He is wearing a pair of glasses that the eye doctor lent him. Thick round ones with silver frames. He looks awful, like an eyeless alien from outer space.

"How was the funeral?" Kawabe asks. Just as I suspected: Kawabe only came to cram school because he is dying to hear about the funeral.

"How was it?" Yamashita repeats blankly.

"Was it interesting?"

"Of course it wasn't interesting," I snort. "Although I wouldn't know myself."

"Yeah," Yamashita agrees. "It wasn't interesting at all. Everyone wore black, and the chanting was really boring, and my uncles sat around and drank while my aunts ran around like chickens with their heads cut off. And the other kids were all younger than me. They had the nerve to call me Fatso."

"But we call you Pudge," Kawabe says, laughing like a horse so you can see his gums. With his silver glasses gleaming in the dark and that wheezy laugh of his, there's something downright creepy about him.

"How would *you* feel if someone you'd never even met before called you Four-eyes?"

Kawabe stops laughing. "Oh. I see what you mean."

"The funeral itself wasn't anything special. It was just—" Yamashita stops and swallows. "When someone dies, they burn them. They take the body to what they call a crematorium, and the coffin is slipped into this great big oven and then—*bang!*—the door is shut. And . . ."

"And?" I prompt him, leaning forward because Yamashita's voice has gotten quieter and quieter.

"And an hour later all that's left is bones and ashes. Everything else is gone. Little pieces of white bone. Just a few little pieces. There were hardly any."

"They burn the body for a whole *hour*?"

"Mmm."

"It must be really hot. The fire must be roaring."

Yamashita thinks for a minute. "There was a great big chimney but only a little trickle of white smoke. My dad said they use electric heat to burn the corpse and it doesn't make as much smoke as the old way. They burn it slowly, bit by bit."

Kawabe starts jiggling, which is a bad sign. Whenever he gets excited or upset, he jiggles his leg up and down like the needle on a sewing machine. If he's standing, he bounces up and down on his toes and his whole body shakes. It's like the switch on a time bomb that could go off any minute, and there's no telling what he might do next. My mom says that Kawabe is eccentric. Maybe she's right.

"Everybody picks the bones out with chopsticks and puts them in an urn."

"With chopsticks?" Kawabe asks.

"Yeah. And then it's over."

And then it's over. But . . .

"Did you cry?" I ask.

"Nah."

"But she was your grandmother. Weren't you sad?"

"I hadn't seen her since I was a baby. She was like a stranger."

"Oh."

"And I had never been to visit her. It was too far."

Come to think of it, I haven't seen my grandmother on my father's side for a very long time either. What does she look like?

"But never mind that," Yamashita says, his voice sounding hoarse. "Have you guys ever seen a dead person?"

"Are you kidding? Course not," Kawabe snorts, and then sinks into silence, his nostrils quivering. Even when I first heard that Yamashita had gone to a funeral, and even when he told us about the bones, it had never occurred to me that he might have seen a real *dead* person.

"Did you?" I ask.

"Mmm." He nods, looking straight at me. So that's what had been on his mind all day when he was gazing

off into space.

"Everyone threw flowers into the coffin. That's when I saw."

"Saw what?" Kawabe's eyes gleam with excitement behind his glasses. "What? What? What? What? What?! Hurry up! Out with it!" he demands, grinding the heels of his sneakers into the ground in his impatience.

"Well, it wasn't really anything," Yamashita says hesitantly. "I did see some cotton stuffed in her ears and up her nose, though."

"In her ears? What for?" Kawabe's legs start jiggling again. "Cotton in her ears and nose . . . Cotton in her ears and nose . . ."

"Kawabe! Shut up a minute, will you!" I growl.

Kawabe stops jabbering but is still jiggling so much that the whole bench rattles.

"So I threw in some chrysanthemums along with everyone else. But—"

A lady waiting for the bus on the bench next to ours is looking at us in a strange way. I press down hard on Kawabe's shoulder.

"The petals scattered in the air and one of them spun slowly down and landed on my grandmother's face. Right on her nose."

A yellow petal, I think to myself, for some reason.

"I wanted to brush it off for her. But I was too scared. And then someone closed the lid of the coffin. They nailed it shut. With a stone for a hammer. *Clunk. Clunk . . .*"

"Ha! You mean that's all?" Kawabe scoffs, and then laughs weakly. His voice is shaking as much as his legs, even though he's trying to laugh it off.

11

"Kawabe, shut up," I snap.

"That night I had a dream," Yamashita continues, and then falls silent.

"A nightmare?" I prompt.

"Mmm . . . You know my big stuffed tiger?"

"Yeah."

"When I was little I used to play pro-wrestling with that tiger. Quite often actually."

I start to say, "Bet you still do," but think better of it.

"In my dream, me and my tiger were wrestling. But suddenly I realized that it wasn't my toy at all . . . It was my grandmother's *corpse*."

"Wa-ha-ha-ha!" Unable to contain himself any longer, Kawabe bursts out laughing. Yamashita glances at him but continues without paying any attention to him.

"Her corpse was just like my toy. It didn't respond at all. When I kicked it, it was all limp and flabby. It didn't say anything or make any noise. It was just a thing. A *thing*."

"A thing."

Yamashita nods. "And that was what was so scary."

Just listening is starting to give me the creeps, even though I've seen plenty of killing and dying on TV and in comic books.

"I wonder what happens when we die," I say. "Is that the end? Or maybe—?"

"There are ghosts," Yamashita says, his face tense. "I used to think that they were light and airy. But now . . ."

12 "But now?"

"They're heavy. I'm sure of it. Very, very heavy. As heavy as a sandbag."

If, as Yamashita was saying, a dead person is just a thing, then ghosts must be things, too. Material, not like spirits or souls, but something you can weigh, like salt, or a tape recorder, or a book. I never want to see the scales when a ghost gets on them.

"I'm scared, you guys, really scared! I wish I had never gone to that funeral," Yamashita blurts out, kicking the ground savagely with the toe of his sneaker.

Kawabe suddenly leaps onto the bench and draws himself up tall. The lady on the bench next to ours clutches her purse tightly to her chest and backs away. Laughing like a maniac, Kawabe yells, "I am immortal!"

For some time after that we don't talk about Yamashita's grandmother. Yamashita is his old self again, and Kawabe, after his strange fit at the bus stop, seems a little subdued but normal otherwise. It's as though we have forgotten about the funeral.

The day Kawabe wears his new glasses to school for the first time, he summons us to meet him in the parking lot of his apartment building after school.

"So what's up?" I ask. He seems so excited it makes me feel uneasy.

"Well . . . Look, you know the calligraphy school? Near where you turn to get to the bus stop?"

"You mean the one near the Negishi Apartments?" I ask. There are a bunch of old rental houses near there that look as if modern times have passed them by. A bunch of wooden bungalows, which you couldn't call

13

nice even if only in flattery, all jammed together on a small plot of land.

"An old man lives alone two houses over from the calligraphy school."

"Hmmm."

Kawabe looks expectantly from one to the other of us. Yamashita, who seems to feel as uneasy as I do, hasn't said a word so far.

"So?" I say bluntly.

"What do you mean 'So'? I heard my mom talking to our neighbor. She said the old man who lives there will probably drop dead soon."

I can't figure out what Kawabe is driving at.

"Kiyama, you've never seen a dead person, right?"

"Right."

"Neither have I."

"What has that got to do with it?"

"Look." Kawabe's eyes are shining in a creepy way. "What do you think will happen if that old man living alone suddenly keels over and dies one day?"

"What will happen? If he dies all by himself?" What would happen, I wonder. All alone without friends or family. If he spoke a few last words, if no one was there to hear them, would the words hover in the air and then vanish? As if he hadn't said anything at all? Even words like "I don't want to die," "It hurts," and "It was a good life"?

"We will get to see him die!" Kawabe exclaims triumphantly.

"Huh?"

"When he dies all by himself. We'll be there to see it."

"We?"

"Of course!"

"Me? No way!" Yamashita shouts. "I'm going home." But Kawabe deftly grabs him by the collar and won't let him go.

"But you have to come. You're the only one who has actually seen a dead person."

"I won't! I won't! I won't!"

"Listen, Yamashita, we are going to spy on the old man. And you are the only one who can tell us if he is really ready to drop dead."

Poor Yamashita looks like he is going to burst into tears.

"What are you talking about!" I say in disgust. No doubt about it—Kawabe is definitely weird. "Vultures hover around a dying animal waiting for it to die so they can feast on its flesh. What are you? Some kind of vulture? That's sick!"

Kawabe seems suddenly deflated. He hangs his head and releases his hold on Yamashita's collar. Yamashita gasps and coughs hoarsely.

"You know," Kawabe whispers, "I keep dreaming about your grandmother. Ever since that time. I've never even met her, but in my dream she falls on top of me. She's so heavy I can't move. Or sometimes I suddenly open my eyes and find fire all around me. And I'm burning in this small narrow place like a tunnel. I scream, 'Help! I'm still alive!' and then I wake up."

I sigh. Although not exactly the same, I have been having similar dreams every night.

"These days all I can think about is dead people," Kawabe continues. "Or about when I am going to die,

15

and what happens when we die. But even though I know in my head that everyone dies sometime, I just can't believe it."

"Me, too," Yamashita and I say in unison.

"You see?" Kawabe says, looking at us more cheerfully. "And when you try to think about something that you can't believe but that you know is true, don't you feel all strange, sort of antsy and grumpy?"

"Yeah, I guess," I say.

"Well, I can't stand it anymore. The teacher told us that we human beings progress because we have the desire to know. Well, I've finally realized at the age of twelve that I have the same desire. When I was crossing the bridge over the railway tracks yesterday . . . I climbed up onto the railing."

Yamashita swallows loudly.

"A train was rushing down the tracks toward me. I thought, If I fall now, the train will hit me and I will die for sure. And I had this jittery feeling that I couldn't stay there without falling."

In my mind I can hear the shrill warning of the train whistle.

"But then I remembered you guys. Even if I did find out what happens when we die, how could I tell you about it if I was dead?" He's suddenly seized by another of his laughing fits. "When I got down off that railing, I actually wet my pants!"

I look at Kawabe with new respect. He is definitely a little strange, but he's also a lot braver than I am. If you really want to know something, then you have to try and find out, no matter how scared you are.

"All right," I say.

"All right what?" Yamashita asks nervously.

I avoid Yamashita's accusing eyes. "But only on condition that it doesn't bother the old man."

"No!" Yamashita explodes.

"Yes! Two against one!" Kawabe shouts gleefully, and he dances a little jig.

2

The house looks as though no one has ever taken care of it. Half the wooden siding is coming off, flapping in the wind. A piece of newspaper is taped over a broken windowpane. The place is surrounded by piles of unidentifiable junk, bundles of old newspapers, bags of garbage, and a big pickling vat that looks like it hasn't been used in years and is now filled with rainwater. On the south side of the house a narrow porch faces onto a small garden with a large fragrant olive bush. Glass doors with opaque glass on the bottom half separate the house from the garden outside.

We can't see through to the back of the house, but the pale-blue light of a television flickers through the glass porch doors. Although it will soon be July, the old man is sitting on the floor at a kotatsu, a low table with a built-in electric heater and a quilt draped over the top. It isn't that hot yet, perhaps because it's been raining every day, but somehow the sight of the red kotatsu quilt pushed up against the glass doors depresses me.

"He's still alive," Kawabe says, standing on tiptoe and peering over the mossy concrete block wall.

I crouch down out of sight behind the wall. "Kawabe, spying requires perseverance. You got that?"

"Yeah, that's right," Yamashita chimes in. "It's a lot harder than it looks on those TV detective shows, you know."

"Of course I know," Kawabe says. "After all, my dad was a detective. Although he told me not to tell anyone."

"Wow!" Yamashita looks at him in admiration. "Neat!"

"Yup. He helped solve some murders that even the *police* couldn't figure out."

"No kidding!"

"You remember the case of the barbershop murders? The ones where the victims were cut to pieces with a pair of scissors?"

"No, I never heard of it."

"Well, it was my father who solved that case. It was a record that gave him the clue he needed. The murderer always played a particular waltz when he killed his victims. My father returned alone to the scene of the crime. It was night. The smell of blood still lingered in the empty barbershop. He placed the needle on the record and . . ."

Much impressed, Yamashita is completely absorbed

in Kawabe's tale. It has started to sprinkle again, but we don't open our umbrellas yet.

Kawabe has no father. He died when Kawabe was a baby. But Kawabe makes up lots of stories about him. Once he claimed that his father was a baseball player, another time a writer, and another time an airplane pilot. He only does it two or three times a year, and usually people just say "Really?" and forget about it, and because our classmates change every year, he usually manages to stay out of trouble. But for someone like me, who has been with him since kindergarten, it's more like "Oh no, here we go again!" And then there are always a few creeps with long memories.

Like last year, when we were practicing for the school talent show. Kawabe was dying for the leading role in the class play, but Sugita stole the part from him. The teacher was supposed to choose the actor for the lead, but before he got around to it Sugita nominated himself, insisting before the entire class that he just had to have that role, and he pushed until he got it. Kawabe was really upset. That's probably why he began to tell everyone that his father had been an actor.

"He was a talented supporting actor. He refused to be on TV programs or anything like that. He only played the stage."

I clearly remember the vicious gleam in Sugita's eyes.

"Kawabe, I thought you said your dad was a pilot." Before Kawabe could find his tongue, Sugita called him a liar. "Ha! So that's what your father really did for a living? He was a measly actor? No wonder you were too embarrassed to tell us."

I'll never forget Kawabe's face. He was furious.

Grinding his teeth, he glared at Sugita so hard that I thought his glasses would fly off his chalk-white face. Even his customary jiggling was stilled.

I feel a little guilty when I remember that incident, because when Kawabe leaped at Sugita, I grabbed him from behind and held him back. I was sure that Kawabe was going to kill Sugita if I didn't stop him. Just the thought of it scared me so much that every pore in my body seemed to shrink shut. What a coward I was. I should have punched Sugita myself, right in the nose, as hard as I could.

That was when Kawabe and I became real friends. A little later Yamashita joined us and our trio was formed. Four-eyes Kawabe, chubby Yamashita, and me. Once we all went over to my house to do homework together. When my mother talked to Kawabe, he couldn't stop jiggling, and then Yamashita spilled juice on the sofa. It was terrible. After they left, my mom said, "Next time maybe you could bring over some better friends." I never brought anyone home after that.

"A detective. Gee, you're lucky!" Yamashita is smiling, his eyes half shut, completely lost in a dream world. He's probably imagining himself as a private eye in a trench coat with a hat pulled down low over his eyes.

"Let's figure out our schedules," I say, squatting on the ground. I put up my umbrella and Yamashita and Kawabe join me underneath it. The rain is falling harder. "From Monday to Friday, we'll go home after school, get our stuff, and meet here on the way to cram school."

"What about baseball?" Yamashita asks.

"We're detectives, right?" Kawabe says. "Besides, 21

you always have to play outfield. Which do you choose, the outfield or being a detective?"

"Which one?" Yamashita repeats.

"Yeah. Which one?"

"Detective, I guess."

"Of course detective!"

"Right," Yamashita agrees reluctantly.

"As for Saturdays—" I continue, but Yamashita interrupts me.

"I . . ." he begins, looking uncomfortable.

"What? What is it?"

"I have to help out in the shop on Saturdays or I'll get in trouble," he finishes. Yamashita's family runs a fish store.

"Hey, that reminds me," Kawabe says. "Kiyama, you and I have swimming on Saturdays."

"Okay, then. Yamashita doesn't have to come on Saturdays, and you and I will come after swimming, which ends at four."

"Okay."

"What about Sunday?"

"We have soccer practice and sometimes tests at cram school. What should we do?"

"If there's a test, it depends on what time it's held. It's different some weeks, so we'll decide on Saturday."

"Great!" Kawabe nods, grunting in satisfaction. "You know, if you think about it, except for swimming, the three of us are together most of the time. Is that weird?" Then he suddenly exclaims, "Wait!" and points at me. "What about piano?"

"I quit. A long time ago," I say, trying to avoid that topic. My mother had made me take piano lessons. I had hated practicing, but now the big silent piano sitting smack in the middle of our house makes me feel guilty. "The teacher had a baby and she went kind of funny, hysterical or something."

"Must be her husband's fault," Kawabe said, sounding like a gossipy middle-aged woman.

"You think so?"

"Yeah. It takes two to raise kids without going crazy. But wait! You mean—"

"What?"

"Did your teacher get married?"

"Yeah. What about it?"

"But you told me that *you* were going to marry her."

"Shut up!"

Kawabe has an excellent memory for strange details like that. I haven't said that since I was in kindergarten.

"Here comes the bride!" Kawabe leaps out into the rain singing the opening bars of "The Wedding March" and shouts, "Teacher, will you marry me?" Yamashita is laughing like crazy. My ears are burning. I can't even play "The Wedding March" on the piano.

They are always together. One is tall and thin, the other short and fat, a typical comic duo. Their hair sticks out all over the place like broom bristles and their eyes glow.

I don't know why the ghosts that haunt me take this form, but when I was little I often dreamed that these two were chasing me. As I'd walk along a dimly lit corridor, I would see their shadows stretching out on the floor as if they were waiting for me. Or they would come chasing after me, shrieking with laughter, down a

23

wide-open road under a leaden sky, the tall one swaying backward and forward, his body stiff and straight as an oar, and the short fat one bouncing along like a balloon. Despite their ridiculous appearance they were terrifying. The more they laughed, the more frightened I became. So frightened sometimes that I wet the bed.

They have been reappearing ever since I heard about Yamashita's grandmother. In the pitch dark they chase after me, laughing wildly, eyes glittering, with pine torches in their hands to set me on fire.

Every night when I wake in a sweat I feel a little ashamed to be frightened of such a childish dream. But unlike when I was younger, at least now I understand a little why the ghosts scare me. It's because they don't care about me one bit. They have no desire to try to understand me and I am sure that I will never understand them. No matter how much I plead, "I don't want to die yet. Please don't kill me," my words have no effect on them. They live in a different world. A world separate from the world I live in. The world of death.

They just chase me. Nothing more. Without even understanding my fear. And I think that's what scares me most of all.

Every day we go to the house, and every day the old man is still sitting at the kotatsu watching TV.

"Must be nice to watch as much TV as you want. I'm only allowed to watch an hour and a half a day," Yamashita says, sitting down by the wall. "Then again, if that's all you had to do with your life, maybe it would be boring."

"Yeah, you're probably right," I agree.

"I'd rather play some computer games, too."

"Yamashita!"

"What?"

"That's why you're so fat," I chide him.

"You mean I should exercise more, right?"

"No. It's just that you take things too easy."

Kawabe is still peering over the concrete-block wall toward the house. He never sits down on the ground like me and Yamashita. "Hmmm. I wonder. You know, maybe that old man died with the television on. Just sitting at the kotatsu. Can you say for sure that he isn't dead?"

Yamashita and I stand up abruptly and peer over the wall. Being the tallest, I don't need to stretch, but Yamashita, who is even shorter than Kawabe, can barely see over even when standing on tiptoe.

"Impossible," Yamashita exclaims, jumping up and down to get a better view.

"I bet that's just what happened," Kawabe says, moving away from the wall for the first time. "Sitting at a kotatsu in this stinking hot weather. No matter how you look at it . . ."

Yamashita quits jumping. Come to think of it, the rain *did* stop today and it *is* starting to get hot and muggy. I stare at the old man's back on the other side of the opaque glass pane where he sits at the kotatsu watching TV as usual. His balding head, the brown shirt he wears, are completely still. Only the light from the TV screen moves.

"Kiyama!"

I turn and notice that Kawabe's eyes have that dangerous glint again. "Your glasses are crooked," I point out, and Kawabe straightens them, but it doesn't stop the gleam in his eyes.

"Let's check it out."

"Hey now, wait a minute," I protest.

"He might be dead. In fact, I'm sure he's dead."

"What are you going to do if he's alive?"

"Well, what are you going to do if he's dead? If you just leave him there, it'll be much worse."

"Yamashita," I say, and Yamashita jumps. "What do you think? Do you think he's dead?"

"Are you kidding?"

"No, he's not kidding," Kawabe says. "You've seen a dead person before, right?" He corners Yamashita. "So smarten up, Pudge."

Yamashita's eyes flick back and forth, looking for help. "I don't know! But . . ."

"But what?"

"If you leave a body lying around, after a while it will start to rot. Maggots will hatch in the rotten flesh and start to munch till it's all gooey and oozing."

Kawabe's legs start to jiggle. We have to act soon or there'll be trouble again.

"Hey, do you smell something?"

"Huh?" Yamashita jumps about three inches.

"Take a whiff. It stinks. I thought something smelled funny. Can it be . . ." Kawabe moves his head from side to side and sniffs, his nostrils flaring. "Yup. That must be it."

Now that he mentions it, there does seem to be a strange smell. A sharp, sour kind of odor.

"Is it . . . *him*?" My voice cracks.

Kawabe nods.

"Let's go home," Yamashita says in a tiny voice, but we ignore him. Kawabe and I are just about to peer over the fence again when there is a slight noise from the house. Then the door right beside the wall suddenly bursts open.

There is a loud scream. I don't know who it is. Probably all three of us. We take off as fast as our legs can go.

When we reach the parking lot of Kawabe's apartment block, gasping for breath, Kawabe says, "Did you see him?" We shake our heads. "Idiots!" he shrieks in frustration, but when Yamashita asks, "Well, did *you*?" he falls silent.

We continue with our detective work. Our investigation reveals that the old man is definitely alive, that he goes shopping every three days at the local convenience store, and that the bags of garbage surrounding his house are the source of the pungent odor of decay. By the time we uncover that much, it is already July, and our school is now on half days, working up to the summer holiday. The only thing that has changed is the weather. It has become unbearably hot. The shabby old man is still alive, and it is very unlikely that any murderer on the "most wanted" list is going to take refuge in his house. I've decided that I'm never going to be a detective when I grow up. Considering the amount of time and patience you need, it's very boring work.

I think the only things that keep me at it are Kawabe's insistence and my own nightmares. Plus, there really isn't anything more interesting to do.

We tail the old man to the convenience store. We go

in to buy ice cream and use that as a cover to check the contents of his shopping basket. He always buys pretty much the same stuff: ready-made lunches, bread, bananas, pickles, canned sardines, instant miso soup, and instant noodles. Although he always buys ready-made lunches, he sometimes skips some of the other things. Occasionally he buys toilet paper.

Then he walks home slowly, carrying his shopping bag. Sometimes he stops and stares at a telephone pole or an empty can, or a sign or someone walking by. It's never a very friendly stare, but more like he's saying, "So what's it to you?" But I don't think it really has any meaning. He stops at the little park where kids from the apartment complex play and eats one banana. Then he stares at the kids playing in the sandbox or at the cat poop in the sand with his "So what's it to you?" stare, and gets slowly to his feet and begins walking home. It is always the same route. He never talks to anybody and no one talks to him.

"He doesn't eat very well, does he?" Yamashita remarks. The old man just came back from the convenience store, so we take up our surveillance positions by the wall again.

"Huh?"

"The old man. He usually eats ready-made lunches, right? Probably one in the evening and one the next morning."

"And you'd probably eat both at once," Kawabe teases him. Yamashita scowls at him for a moment, then grudgingly admits that he might. He folds his plump arms and gazes upward in thought.

"My mom works late so we always eat ready-made

stuff for supper. I know the shops around here pretty well," Kawabe says. "The takeout meals at Ginshari-tei a little farther down are a lot better than the convenience store ones. Then there is always sushi from Kyotaru. Of course, it closes early."

"We always have fish that didn't sell," Yamashita says.

"We even eat store-bought meals on Sundays. They're a lot better than my mom's cooking."

"Really?" My mom stays home all day. And she cooks for me and my dad all the time. When I come home late after cram school, she fries me up a steak. Then she watches me eat every bite. I don't really like her staring at me while I eat, but I don't say so. While she watches, she nibbles on a cracker or something and drinks wine.

My dad usually comes home right after I finish dinner but sometimes even later. My mom goes back into the kitchen. But my dad only eats something simple like rice with hot green tea poured over it. My mom doesn't eat with my dad. Sometimes I wonder if she eats at all.

3

I keep having trouble remembering what the old man looks like. When I see him on the street, I recognize him immediately. Yet when I return home and try to recall his face, I can only come up with a fuzzy image.

The old man always wears the same brown shirt and sloppy dark-gray pants held up with a belt. He wears a pair of gym shoes and carries a shopping bag. He is very thin and half bald. Those kinds of general features I can recall, along with some smaller details like the liver spots on his hands, but whenever I try to picture his face, somehow I can't.

"Me neither," Yamashita says in surprise when I tell him. "I'll be watching a TV show about some old guy who used to be the boss of a robber gang but is now hiding out making pipes or something, and I'll think, Ah, that guy looks like the old man. But then I'll see a different actor on another show and think, No, wait a minute. He looks more like this guy here."

"Me too," Kawabe says. "I heard somewhere that it's hard to remember the face of the girl you love."

Yamashita chokes on the juice he's drinking. "How did that old man suddenly turn into some girl we like?" Such a comeback is unusual for him.

"I don't mean that he's a girl we like—"

"He sure isn't!"

"But why can't we remember his face?"

"Maybe it's because we're only sneaking a peek at him," Yamashita suggests.

"That could be it," I say. Kawabe remains silent as though this answer is unsatisfactory. In fact, I'm not satisfied with it myself.

"Ah!"

The door rattles open. It's made of cheap plywood, so it can't help but rattle.

We quickly hide behind a parked car and begin to tail the old man. He walks slowly as usual, dragging his feet a little. We know his destination must be the convenience store, so you would think we would just go there ahead of him. But no, we respect Kawabe's instructions to do this properly and stalk him like secret agents, hiding behind telephone poles and vending machines.

The old man reaches the local shopping area, a narrow street lined with shops. As he turns the corner, he glances behind him suddenly. Startled, Yamashita bumps his head on a telephone pole. The old man looks thoughtful and then disappears.

"Clumsy oaf!" Kawabe growls. "Now we're ruined."

"Ruined?"

"Now he knows your face. And even without that, you stick out." He doesn't say "because you're fat," but he doesn't need to.

Yamashita looks at the ground. His eyes are blinking rapidly.

"Don't start crying, Pudge. Disguise yourself."

"Huh?"

"I said, disguise yourself." Kawabe pulls a square red box from his pocket. "I knew this would come in handy someday."

Inside the plastic case is something black and spiky that looks like a centipede, and a tube of glue.

"It's a fake mustache. Put it on."

Yamashita begins to protest and fidget, but Kawabe ignores him and starts to open the glue.

"Cut it out." For once I'm on Yamashita's side. A chubby elementary-school kid sporting a little black mustache would be even more conspicuous. "Come on! Let's go to the convenience store."

"To the convenience store!" Yamashita yells, dashing off before I even start running.

The old man isn't in the convenience store, but we don't worry about it and set off for the park instead. Then we realize he isn't there either.

"I guess he did figure out that he was being followed," Yamashita mutters uncomfortably.

I decide to take charge. "So let's try and find him. Yamashita, you check out his house and the surrounding neighborhood. Kawabe, you take the shopping area. Let's meet back here in thirty minutes."

"Roger."

We break up and set off like seasoned members of the secret service.

I have a hunch: the big hospital up the road from the park. I run up the hill, imagining how impressed Yamashita and Kawabe will be when I find him.

The late-afternoon sun floods through the large skylight in the waiting room. There's a receptionist, a cashier, and a pharmacy, and past them many small corridors with signs pointing to the X-ray room, and the internal medicine, pediatrics, ophthalmology, orthopedics, surgery, and obstetrics departments.

I take a quick glance around the central waiting room to confirm that the old man is not there and then check out the waiting areas for each department. There are very few old people; instead, there are a lot of mothers with children and people who look like they left work a little early.

I have been here before. It was the day I woke up with my eye bright red like the eye of a dead fish. "Must be pinkeye," my mother had said. "We'd better go see the doctor." I told her I could go by myself, but she insisted on coming with me. So I took the day off from school and came here in the morning. The waiting room had been full of old people and pregnant women.

While we waited, we heard the doctor's shrill voice from within his office. "But I just gave you some eye medicine yesterday! How could it be gone already? Now tell me the truth! Why is the medicine I gave you yesterday already gone?!" There was a muffled response, and then the doctor started in again: "You spilled it?! Why did you spill it? What's that? You didn't do it on purpose? On purpose!" The sound of his voice made me jump. It was just like a police detective cross-examining a witness. I was sure that the patient would be a kid like me, but when the door opened, a shriveled old man came out. He carried his wallet in a plastic shopping bag, his face was blotchy, and his shirt hung halfway out of his trousers. When his eyes met mine, he smiled sheepishly. I will never forget that old man's face.

Then it was my turn. The doctor smiled at my mother and said, "He has conjunctivitis. Make sure he uses a separate towel and washbasin from the rest of the family. He'll be fine. I'll prescribe some excellent medicine. It should clear up within five days." On the way home my mother said, "Well, that was lucky. We got a good doctor, didn't we?" I thought about the man he'd yelled at and felt kind of sick to my stomach.

I'm startled out of my memory by the sound of a siren. It might be the old man! I rush through the waiting room to the entrance, but the stretcher has already been carried into the building.

"Fell down the stairs, they said." A middle-aged woman in a hospital gown is talking to a visitor. My feet carry me toward her and stop in front of her.

"Uh, excuse me." My voice is hoarse.

"Yes?" The skin around her eyes is horribly swollen like the seedpods of some creepy kind of plant.

"The person who just came in the ambulance, was it an old man?"

"No. An old woman."

I'm so relieved that I forget to thank her.

Kawabe and Yamashita are already waiting for me by the time I return to our meeting place.

"Any luck?" Kawabe's legs are jiggling again. When I shake my head, he narrows his eyes and says, "So he gave us the slip."

"Oh, come on. This is not some detective show."

From there we search the public bath, the putting range, the department store, and a model-home exhibition we would never have visited otherwise. By the time we decide to take one more look at his house, it's completely dark and our feet are killing us from so much walking. The lights are on.

"Well, what do you know? He came home," Yamashita says, and sinks to the ground in exhaustion. Kawabe and I slump down beside him and the three of us lean our backs against the wall and stare off into space.

"Why did we kill ourselves trying to find him?"

"Yeah. What idiots," Kawabe says, and then gives a short laugh. A crow is cawing even though the sun has already set. The rush of the expressway in the distance sounds like a peaceful river flowing. I'm getting sleepy.

Yamashita suddenly gives a wild shriek. "Oh no!"

"What now?"

"Cram school! We forgot!"

We have never forgotten cram school before. We leap to our feet. I lean forward to peer at Yamashita's wristwatch just as he leans forward to look at Kawabe's and Kawabe to look at mine, and we all smack our heads together.

"It'll be finished in half an hour. What should we do?"

"Let's skip it," Kawabe says.

"You—you think so?" Yamashita says nervously.

"Let's go anyway," I say.

"Kiyama the goody-goody," Kawabe says. Yamashita's face is a mixture of disappointment and relief.

"Well, I'm going." I'm a bit annoyed at being called a goody-goody.

"Are you serious?"

"You heard me."

We start walking. Yamashita tries to soothe Kawabe, who keeps on complaining, "Aw come on, there's no point in going now. Let's skip cram school."

The last Saturday of the first school term, Yamashita has to help at the store as usual, so Kawabe and I take the evening surveillance shift. Unfortunately for us, the cram school called our parents when we were late the day before and Kawabe is in the dumps because his mother hit him. My mother, on the other hand, just drank and watched me eat. Only this time she drank a lot more than usual. But she didn't say anything.

The two of us peer silently at the old man's house, Kawabe stretching up as high as he can and me bending a little so that the top of my head won't be so visible. I seem to be growing a lot lately. I really notice it now because we spend so much time plastered against this wall. Sometimes the sight of my gawky legs sticking out of my shorts and my even gawkier arms depresses me. No wonder some stupid girls at school call me Beanpole. Even my face seems to have grown longer, especially my nose. I never used to have such a long nose.

"Hey!" someone behind us calls in a hushed voice. It's Yamashita. He must have run all the way. He is drenched with sweat.

"What's up?"

"You shouldn't be playing hooky from work," Kawabe lectures him.

"Here." Yamashita hands us a parcel wrapped in newspaper.

"What is it?"

Yamashita laughs with embarrassed pride and unwraps it. It's sashimi. "Looks good, doesn't it?"

He holds a plastic plate with slices of raw tuna, squid, and sea urchin resting on a bed of dark-green leaves and slivers of transparent daikon radish. I don't really like fish myself, but the stuff on that plate looks beautiful.

"You're delivering somewhere?" I ask.

"I swiped it."

"What for?"

Yamashita seems a little uncomfortable.

"Well, what are you going to do with that fish?" I prod.

"I thought that, well, maybe we should give it to the old man."

"Yamashita! You're brilliant!" Kawabe turns to him with sudden interest. "No, not just brilliant. A genius!"

"Really? Me?" Yamashita says with shy pleasure.

"Sure. After all, if we go on like this, that old man may never die," Kawabe says seriously.

"Huh?"

Kawabe is staring fixedly at the fish. "It doesn't look poisoned, though."

Yamashita whips the plate of sashimi behind his back and growls, "This is no joke, Kawabe!"

"What's your problem?" Kawabe snaps back. "You mean you didn't put poison in it?"

"I j-just thought it might be a nice treat for the old guy!"

Come to think of it, the old man hasn't eaten sashimi even once in all the time we've been shadowing him. Just ready-made and canned food from the convenience store.

"Have you lost your mind! Why do you think we've been going to all the trouble of spying on him every day?" Kawabe glares at Yamashita, his black eyes sharp like the pointed ends of a pair of thumbtacks.

"Well, yeah, I know, but . . ."

"So what's the point in feeding him healthy food, stupid!"

"But . . ." Yamashita stares at his feet, gripping the plate of sashimi tightly. "Something nice to eat isn't going to make that much difference. Not if he's really going to drop dead soon anyway."

Kawabe broods silently, then clucks his tongue in exasperation. "How are you going to give it to him?" he asks suddenly.

"I'll put it by the door and knock. Then I'll hide," Yamashita answers confidently. It's obvious that he's been thinking it over for some time.

"Then why don't you go ahead and do it?" Kawabe says.

Yamashita looks at me uncertainly. "By myself?"

"Of course. It was your idea," Kawabe snaps. Yamashita is still looking at me.

"It would probably be quieter if you did it alone, don't you think?" I say.

Yamashita looks miserable.

"I think it's a nice idea, you know," I say.

"You do?"

"Yes, I do."

Yamashita looks steadily at the door. Then he looks at me and, at my nod, reaches through a gap in the wall and gently slips the plate onto the stone step in front of the door. He looks back at us. Kawabe and I wave our arms frantically, gesturing for him to go on. He nods once more, scratches his upper lip, takes two steps forward, and, holding his breath, raps loudly on the door.

"Look out! Here he comes!" we hiss.

We roll away, hiding in the shadow of a nearby car. The door opens and the old man peers outside, bends down, stands up, and closes the door. When we return to look, the plate is gone.

"Do you think he'll eat it?" Yamashita seems a little uncertain. "Maybe he'll think it was poisoned."

"Of course he'll eat it," Kawabe says. "He looks like the type."

"Besides, it looked really delicious," I say.

At that Yamashita collapses on the ground. "Phew!" he sighs. "I thought I was going to have a heart attack!"

It's the first day of the summer holidays, which means we'll be going to cram school every morning instead of at night. There's a lot of grumbling because we have to be there even earlier than for elementary school. We'll begin the day by exercising in time to a radio show and then go on to studying.

The road to the bus stop goes past the old man's house. Because the elementary school lies in the opposite direction, I have never seen his house in the morning before.

He doesn't have the TV on. I can't see his balding head either. He's probably still asleep. The old Japanese proverb that the elderly are early risers is obviously untrue.

A flock of sparrows perches in the fragrant olive bush, twittering merrily. The slanting rays of the early-morning sun shine into the cluttered garden, where a cat sits busily licking an empty container it tore from a plastic garbage bag in front of the house. It's not such a bad view in its own way.

He probably sleeps late all the time and misses garbage collection, I think. I go up to the front of the house and begin gathering up the garbage bags which lie haphazardly about the yard. It's Monday, one of the three weekly garbage days. All I have to do is take them to the collection site about ten yards away. When I pick one up, the stray cat protests loudly. A sickening, sour smell rises from the bags. I feel like throwing up, but control myself. "Hsst! Quiet!" I say to the cat. Question: Why does garbage smell so awful? Answer: Because it is changing. I find this thought curious. All those delicious things like bananas, salmon, and canned sardines eventually begin to rot, making a horrible stench. And if the delicious smell of meat beginning to stew indicates a kind of change, then so do the sweet smell of fermented wine and the odor of food rotting. But I experience these changes as "good smells" or "bad smells." I wonder if there are good changes and bad changes. If so, then the sudden sprouting of my legs and arms must be a bad change.

I take a big whiff of garbage. I almost throw up and my eyes fill with tears. At that moment I hear voices behind me.

"Kiyama, what do you think you're doing?" It's Kawabe and Yamashita. Their heads are poking through the gap in the wall.

41

"I was going to take the garbage out."

"Garbage?" Yamashita's eyes grow large and round.

"What for, you idiot?" Kawabe says. "Come on, get out of there."

"Give me a hand. I can't do it all by myself."

"Have you lost your mind?"

"I think the old man is still asleep."

"Why should we take his garbage out?"

"Because it stinks when we're spying on him. You said so yourself."

"But—"

"Never mind. Just give me a hand, will you?"

The two of them reluctantly step inside the yard. Kawabe stomps right on the tail of the stray cat, which was trying to rub up against him, and it gives a shrill squeal.

"Eek!" Yamashita shrieks.

"Yamashita, keep it down!" I snap, and begin passing garbage bags to both of them as they stand nervously by the wall.

"Phew! It stinks!" Kawabe exclaims, his face wrinkling in disgust.

"Even the newspapers are rotting. This is gross!" Yamashita says, picking up another bag to add to his load.

"Oh well, I guess it won't hurt. After all, in return we get to spy on him." Kawabe seems to have resigned himself to the idea.

"Okay. Let's take them to the garbage collection site," I am saying when the door suddenly opens with a vigorous bang. Turning around, I smack my forehead right into the door.

"All right! What are you up to?"

For an instant everything goes blank and I stare stupidly, not understanding what is going on.

"I said, what are you doing?" The old man, wearing only a shrunken undershirt and underpants, is standing right in front of me. I have never seen his face this close before. It's shaped like a fava bean, and his eyes are like little black dots. They flick nervously back and forth, contrasting with his stern voice. His teeth are yellow, or maybe brown, and he is missing two bottom teeth, one on either side of the front four, and his right incisor on top. White stubble flecked with black bristles around his face, in sharp contrast to his shiny, balding head. I stare at him dumbly, unable to tear my gaze away. Our eyes meet and I give a start.

"The garbage . . ." I finally say.

"Garbage?" The old man looks us over carefully. Kawabe and Yamashita stand frozen, garbage bags still clutched in their hands.

"We just thought it might be a good idea to take the garbage out."

"You kids have been hanging around a lot lately, haven't you?"

I am startled. "Not really . . . It's just—" Uh-oh, bad move. Why did I have to add on those last words? After all, I can't exactly say, "We were just spying on you so we can see you when you die."

"It's just that we wanted to take your garbage out," I finish lamely.

"Liar!" Then he adds, as if to himself, "Can't take my eyes off you kids even for a second."

That hurts. Because today at least we really were

43

only thinking of taking the garbage out. I wish he could understand that, but at the same time I know that we aren't exactly innocent, so it seems better to remain silent. And because I use my head, I keep quiet. Unfortunately, there are others in this world who do not use their heads at all.

"Are you trying to say that we did something wrong?" It is Kawabe.

"Drop it, Kawabe," Yamashita warns him.

The old man just says "Hmph!" and closes the door.

"Wait! Are you accusing us of stealing or something?"

"Kawabe! Forget it," I say, and grip his shoulder. He is in a dangerous mood.

The old man opens the door. "What kind of attitude is that? And just what were you doing, then, coming into my garden without asking?"

"We're very sorry. We . . ." Yamashita breaks in, but the old man just ignores him and glares at Kawabe.

"I pity your father, to have such a son as you!"

Now we're in for it! Kawabe gets really riled up if you mention his father. His warning system, the jiggling, is already starting.

"My father . . . My father was a fireman. He died trying to save someone from a fire! He was a hero!"

The old man slams the door.

"Hey! Wait a minute! Can't you even listen?! Come back here!" Kawabe screams at the door. There is nothing we can do to stop him now. "Damn! Listen, you stupid old geezer! We were spying on you, you hear? We were spying on you because you're going to die soon. And I'm going to be there to see how you die!"

Yamashita and I grab Kawabe, who is struggling wildly, and drag him out to the road. He suddenly calms down and begins walking. We leave the garbage at the old man's house.

We don't talk at cram school. During a math quiz I gaze absently around the room. Yamashita is hunched over in the seat in front of mine. His pencil barely moves. Beside him Kawabe keeps breaking his pencil lead. The *tap-tap-glide* of pencils on paper, the faint sound of breathing, and the low moan of the air conditioner fill the room. It sounds as though the classroom has sunk to the bottom of a pond.

I hear careful footsteps stop behind my desk. The teacher bends over to look at my answer sheet. I hurriedly pull the test paper toward me.

I'm thinking about the old man. He must surely have heard Kawabe from the other side of the door. I can't forget his eyes, which I saw when I stood so close to him. They were full of doubt and maybe even a little mean, but they remind me of the eyes of Chiro, the dog we had when I was little.

He was a very old dog. So old he didn't even like to go for walks but just lay around in the corner of the garden with bits of poop caked to his bum. Before I was born, when it was just my mother and father, they used to take him to the river and let him run along the bank. I found it hard to believe that he had dashed about ruffled by the wind, so filled with excitement that he couldn't hold his pee. To me he seemed like a dirty old blanket, and since the only attention I ever paid to him was to pull his tail, he would turn himself away from me in disgust whenever I came near. One evening, my mother told me that the vet would come and give the dog an injection early the next morning and that Chiro would be dead before I woke up.

That night I sat beside him. He didn't even have the energy to turn away from me but just stared at me with his big black eyes. He seemed anxious. And I could understand how he felt, because I was uneasy, too. I had an inexplicable feeling that something very important was about to leave me behind, and when my mother finally dragged me off to bed, I burst into tears.

The next day the dog was in a cardboard box. My father ordered me not to look inside. Why didn't I insist that I had to see? The dog was buried like that, trapped inside the box. Even now, every time I remember the way Chiro's eyes looked that night, I am overcome by that same sense that I have missed seeing something important.

Cram school finishes in the morning and we sit on the bench at the bus stop, eating bread buns silently. It's the same bench we were sitting on when Yamashita first told us about his dead grandmother.

"Let's go to the pool today," Yamashita says, as though he can't stand it any longer. We are allowed to swim in the school pool for part of the summer holiday, and today is the first day.

"Good idea," I agree.

"How about you, Kawabe?"

Kawabe is methodically stuffing his mouth with a bun. When he finally manages to swallow it down, he says gloomily, "I'm not going."

"Why don't you give up this spying business?" Yamashita says uncomfortably. "That old man doesn't look as if he's going to die very soon, anyway."

Kawabe glares fiercely at the ground. Yamashita and I look at each other. Recalling Kawabe's idea of putting poison in the sashimi, I feel a little uneasy.

Kawabe shoves the second bun into his mouth and stands up. We have no choice. We resign ourselves to following him. After all, we know only too well what he might do if left on his own.

The glass doors around the porch are shut tight even though it's boiling outside. Something rattles and a window opens, but as soon as he notices we are there, the old man slams it shut. The next day the window opens again, and just when we think the old man is coming out, he heaves a bucket of water at us with all his might. The water goes splat against the wall, missing us.

"Too bad!" Kawabe jeers.

We continue to tail him to the store, though perhaps "tailing" is not the right word. Kawabe walks stiffly behind him, glaring at his back. He does not even attempt to hide. The old man sometimes stops suddenly and glances back, and we freeze in our tracks.

"It's like playing tag." Yamashita chuckles, but Kawabe gives him a look and Yamashita falls silent.

I wonder why the old man has started eating so much recently. He goes shopping every day now, and not just to the convenience store either. He also buys a few green vegetables at the grocer's and some sashimi at the fish shop.

"That sashimi I gave him must have been really delicious," Yamashita says. "But if he's going to buy some anyway, why doesn't he buy it at our shop?"

Kawabe clicks his tongue. "I guess you should have poisoned it, after all. Stupid old man!"

We lose sight of him again one evening in the local shopping area. As before, we split up. I am running through the crowded street when I bump into Kawabe.

"Did you spot him?" Kawabe asks. When I shake my head, Kawabe falls into step beside me.

"He'll probably just go home, anyway, so we may as well go back to the house," I suggest.

Kawabe doesn't say anything. It's really muggy. It looks like there's a shower coming and the old man will probably head for home. I'm sure he wasn't carrying an umbrella, I am thinking to myself when Kawabe interrupts my thoughts.

"My father," he begins.

"Yeah?"

"He's not dead."

I look at Kawabe. He is staring straight ahead through the crowds of people thronging the shopping street.

"He's got kids, other kids besides me. And those kids have a mother. Not my mother," he says, and then he whispers, "Die." I can't tell if he's talking to the women shopping for their dinners, the old man, his father, the other kids, or the other mother. "I'm sorry I lied."

"It's okay." I never expected him to apologize.

"Kiyama!" Yamashita is waving at us. "Over here! Over here!"

The old man is in front of the post office. He's leaning against the mailbox and looking around.

"Do you think he's looking for someone?" Yamashita asks, watching him carefully.

"For who?" Kawabe starts walking toward the old man, but stops suddenly.

It doesn't look like anyone is coming. When he glances around once more, the old man's eyes fall on me. And he sets off at a brisk pace.

"You don't suppose," Yamashita says as he runs to catch up with Kawabe, "that he might have been waiting for us?"

"Of course not, stupid."

Of course not. Of course not, but . . . Yamashita is looking at me. I shrug. Who knows?

The next day we take up our posts as usual beside the wall beneath the merciless sun. Our brains have been completely fried by the heat, but the old man has still not appeared at the window. The television isn't on either. Thinking that perhaps he went shopping early, we wait some more. Over an hour passes, but still he doesn't come home.

"Maybe he collapsed inside the house," Yamashita says anxiously.

"It's too sudden. He seemed perfectly fine yesterday," I say.

"My grandmother went like that. They said that the day before she died she was cooking up a storm."

Another hour passes, but not even the slightest sound comes from the house. Kawabe presses his lips tightly together and stares at the window. His gaze moves slowly over to the door and then back to the window again. He has been jiggling for some time. "Get hold of yourself!" I snap, but my voice is shaking.

49

The sound of the cicadas is very loud. They are probably in the fragrant olive bush. A car drives by behind us. Then it's the cicadas again.

"You know," Kawabe says in a small voice, "I blow up real easy and say things I don't mean."

I want to tell him not to worry about it, but the words stick in my throat. I know it will be impossible for him not to worry.

"I've always had bad eyesight, ever since I was a little kid. That's why I'm so short-tempered."

"What does bad eyesight have to do with a short temper?" I demand.

"I wish I had apologized." Kawabe's face twists.

"Maybe we should knock," Yamashita says fearfully. At that moment the window rattles and slides open about a foot. We hold our breath and stare. The old man's thin spotted hand appears, trembling feebly. Like the hand of a zombie crawling from beneath a gravestone.

"What should we do? He must be dying!" Yamashita dithers about, still standing on tiptoe.

"What do you mean, what should we do?" I snap.

"What should we do? What should we do?"

Kawabe's body goes rigid, his eyes open wide, and a strange rumbling noise comes from deep in his throat.

"Kawabe!" I say sharply. I don't know what I should be looking at, that old zombie hand or Kawabe, who looks like he's about to start foaming at the mouth. I keep turning my head from one to the other like a chicken.

"Huh?" The old man's hand has stopped fluttering. And then suddenly he raises the index and middle fingers of his hand in a V. The victory sign. Aimed directly at us.

"Stupid old geezer! Thinks he can fool around with us, does he?!" You can almost see the steam rising from Kawabe, he's so mad.

"He's making fun of us!" I'm mad myself. That old man had me really worried.

"You know, I think he's playing a game with us," Yamashita says, looking both annoyed and like he is going to burst out laughing.

"Shut up!" Kawabe stalks off without even adjusting his glasses, which have slipped down his nose. Yamashita and I run to catch up with him.

"That was definitely a declaration of war," Kawabe says, stopping abruptly and turning on his heel. "I will never give up spying on the old man, you hear me? I don't care what you guys say, even if I have to do it by myself."

"It's okay with me," I say. "If that's the way the old man wants it, let's do it right." Any guilt I have been feeling up to now has completely disappeared. If it's war he wants, then it's war he'll get.

"He's got some nerve," Yamashita remarks. That's true. Even if we did try to kill him, I don't think he would die, just out of spite.

5

The old man is cleaning up the garden. He gathers all the bags stuffed with old newspapers and garbage, the pickling vat, a sandal that has lost its mate, and begins to pile them in front of the house. The sun beats down on his balding head.

It has been really hot lately. Every day, it seems, the cram-school teacher says, "This summer will determine academic victory or defeat. You've got to stick it out." The newspapers are full of photos of beaches jammed with people and articles about children left in cars who died of the heat and ways to avoid getting sick from too much air conditioning. It seems like the same day just repeats over and over again, forever. Everything is being crushed beneath the oppressive summer heat. Perhaps what we are looking for is an escape from the grueling, repetitive days.

We take up our posts beside the wall and watch the old man without even attempting to conceal ourselves. It seems stupid to sneak around, and as for me, it's pretty tiring to stand with my knees bent all the time to keep my head from showing above the wall. I've been growing like crazy. I feel like the beanstalk from *Jack and the Beanstalk,* a curling vine stretching up and up and up.

The old man doesn't throw water at us anymore. He doesn't even tell us to get lost. He moves about, grunting occasionally with the effort, or talking to himself: "Phew! This is hard work." But I somehow feel that if he were really alone he wouldn't be talking out loud.

"He's pretty determined, isn't he," Yamashita says, his eyes just peeping over the wall. He has caught up with Kawabe in height, and if he keeps on growing like that, he'll soon be able to look over the wall easily. "Before he just sat around and watched TV all day, like a living corpse. What's got into him?"

I've been wondering the same thing. Last night, for example, he fried up some tempura. The delicious smell of frying reached all the way out to the wall, making our stomachs rumble.

"He's taunting us," Kawabe says. "He knows we're watching him and that's what's giving him energy. The creep!"

It's true that when you know someone is watching, it can make you try harder. Whenever I'm alone, I don't get very far with my studying. But if I do it at the kitchen table when my mom is cooking, I can really concentrate. My dad gets mad, though, and says, "The kitchen isn't for studying!" and my mom drinks a lot, so I tend to spend a great deal of time in my room these days, even when there's no cram school. I don't like seeing my mother drink. It's as if she's gone someplace else, and that makes me nervous.

"What are you guys doing?"

We turn and see Sugita and Matsushita. This can only mean trouble.

"You're always hanging around that house, aren't you?"

"Not really."

"You can't fool us. What are you doing here? Why don't you ever come to the swimming pool?"

"None of your business."

"Oh yeah?" Sugita says, his pointed chin jutting out a little. "Hey, Fatso." He turns to Yamashita. "It so happens my mom buys fish at your shop."

"S-so? What about it?" Yamashita says in a voice as shrill as a mosquito's whine.

"How 'bout I ask my mom, 'Did you know Yamashita has been peeping into other people's houses?' " Sugita says in a menacing tone. Yamashita pales.

"Ha! A Peeping Tom! That's disgusting!"

"Disgusting!" Matsushita parrots.

"Invasion of privacy," Sugita says.

"Yeah, invasion," Matsushita repeats.

"The police will get you!"

"They'll get you." Matsushita is so stupid.

"I don't suppose you guys are," Sugita lowers his voice, "planning a robbery, or something?"

"What did you say?" Kawabe growls.

"Kawabe, let's go." Yamashita grabs Kawabe's arm. I slide as far away from the wall as I can.

"We were just worried about the old man, that's all," I say. "He lives alone. We help him out sometimes. Take his garbage out and stuff."

"Liar!" Sugita jeers. The old man accused me of the very same thing. I can't think of anything to say.

"What're you doing?" I hear the old man's voice from the other side of the wall. Looking over my shoulder, I see him standing in the middle of the garden with a big tub full of laundry.

"Some new faces, I see. Well, come on in. It's time to hang these up now."

I'm at a loss for words, as if my brain has suddenly shut down. Sugita and Matsushita eye us suspiciously. Sugita's taunting gaze all but says, "It's not *my* problem."

"Coming!" I yell in desperation, and walk straight into the garden, followed by Yamashita and Kawabe. Sugita and Matsushita take off.

"You there, you're the tallest." The old man hands me a thick rope made of rough twine like the kind used for tying parcels. "Tie this tight to that tree over there."

I put one foot on the lowest branch of the fragrant olive bush, wrap the rope around it, and try to tie a knot. I try, but it doesn't work very well. The rope is prickly and I've never tied anything so thick before.

"Okay?" the old man asks.

I grab the rope as tightly as I can and tie a double reef knot. "Okay!"

The old man pulls out a stool to stand on and loops

the middle of the rope around a thick metal hook that supports the gutter. Then he gives me the other end and tells me to tie it to the one remaining pole of what used to be a laundry rack in the other corner of the garden.

"You've got to pull it tight," the old man says, coming over to where I am struggling with the rope. Taking a deep breath, he gives it a yank. He's just a little taller than me. His spotty hands with the bones showing through the skin don't look very strong, but the rope springs perfectly taut and straight. Once on TV I saw fishermen on their boats tying their fishing nets. It's not exactly the same, but the way the old man pulls on that rope reminds me of them.

The rope is now strung in a V shape around the garden. The old man passes the tub of laundry to Yamashita and hands Kawabe some clothespins. I take laundry out of the tub that Yamashita is holding and throw it over the line, while Kawabe fastens it with the pins. When Kawabe can't reach, I pin them on. The clothespins have lain so long in the sun that the plastic is all rough.

"That's no good. You have to stretch the clothes to get the wrinkles out," Kawabe says, snapping smooth the clothes that I had hung up and deftly pinning them. He is very good at it.

"Did you see their faces? Sugita and Matsushita?" Kawabe whispers without stopping his work.

"Yeah, I sure did."

"They looked so stunned when they saw us actually come in here."

"Yeah."

56 "It was funny."

"Yeah, they were really shocked."

"That's not bad," the old man says from his perch on the porch.

"Huh?" I say.

"Not you. The kid with the glasses. I don't know about your schoolwork, but you're sure good at hanging laundry."

Kawabe clicks his tongue, but doesn't really look angry. "It's my job at home. Hanging the laundry," he says to me privately. Probably because his mother works. I have never even imagined Kawabe hanging up laundry.

Three towels, four undershirts with the necks stretched out of shape, two pairs of long underwear and five pairs of underpants with the elastic gone, two pairs of thick socks covered in fluff balls, one hand towel, two sheets, a pair of cotton pants, one pillowcase, and a quilt cover.

"Well, that's all of it. Everything I own has been washed," the old man says with satisfaction when we finish. We have never seen the old man do any laundry before.

The clothesline sags down to eye level, and standing next to it, I can feel the cool, damp, soap-scented breeze sinking into my sweating skin.

"Let's go," Kawabe says. "We've finished. Hurry up."

"Yeah, you're right," I respond, but the thought of standing guard on the other side of the fence again depresses me a bit.

"Hey! Here!" The old man calls out cheerfully from inside the house. "Here," he says coming out onto the porch again. "Take this." And he hands Kawabe a shopping bag that is filled to bursting. We stare at the bag. What could it be? Is it all right to accept it?

"Garbage. There's a pile of it beside the front door."

"Hey, you can't do that!" Kawabe growls, but Yamashita nudges him in the arm.

"Sugita's here again."

"Really?"

"Yeah, I just saw him."

We have no choice. We carry the bag to the front door. There is a huge pile of garbage there already.

"How come he has so much garbage?" Yamashita wonders.

"He's been saving it," I sigh.

"Yeah, and as old as he is, he's saved up a lot."

"Look," Kawabe says, his eyes bright and hard. "Don't talk to that old geezer any more than you have to. He's no friend of ours, got it?"

"Yeah, I know," Yamashita mumbles.

"No, you don't. We're doing this for our reasons only, not for him—"

"What day is it tomorrow?" the old man asks suddenly.

"Friday," Kawabe answers immediately, and then scowls fiercely. Yamashita is grinning.

"A garbage day," the old man says.

"So what!" Kawabe shouts.

6

The next morning we take the garbage out. Kawabe protests to the bitter end, but I finally convince him that it's the right thing to do. It's still bothering me that both Sugita and the old man called me a liar. It takes five trips with the three of us to carry all the garbage from the front of his house to the collection site by the telephone pole.

"Is he still asleep? Cheeky old man." Kawabe peers toward the porch. The windows are shut tight.

After cram school finishes, we hang around beside the wall. Yamashita is saying that if Sugita finds us here again today, he will be in trouble.

"So what are you going to do about it? Give up?" Kawabe says in a gloomy voice.

"We don't really have a choice, do we?"

"Well, I'm not going to!" Kawabe takes up his post by the wall again. "But if you want to quit, go right ahead."

Yamashita looks at me, his face screwed up as though he is about to cry. What should we do? It isn't as if Kawabe isn't nervous, too. Even while peering over the wall he keeps a lookout down the street.

"Let's quit. We could get into trouble," Yamashita starts to plead with Kawabe, when we hear the window on the porch side rattle open.

"With all those weeds out there," the old man remarks in a loud voice, "there are so many mosquitoes that I can't even open the window."

So we start weeding. As we suspected, Sugita and Matsushita come by, but their eyes widen when they see us slaving away and slapping mosquitoes, and they take off.

The old man's garden is overrun with weeds like an abandoned lot. Now that all the garbage is gone, the weeds are particularly noticeable. Sitting on the edge of the porch with a hand towel wrapped around his head, the old man makes comments like "Pull harder," "Make sure you get the roots," and "Come on! Work!"

"Why don't you do it yourself, then," Kawabe mutters under his breath.

But the old man hears him and makes an excuse, saying, "I have bad knees, so I can't bend down."

"For an old man he sure has good hearing," Kawabe declares loudly and distinctly, so that the old man can hear, but this time he pretends not to.

"He's certainly making good use of us," Yamashita says.

"Don't complain. We'll get what we came for," Kawabe responds without even looking at Yamashita. He is dripping with sweat and his glasses have slipped down his nose. No matter how often he pushes them up, they slip down again. Yamashita, maybe because he is fat, keeps losing his balance when he squats. Every time he yanks up a weed, he falls down hard on his bottom. It's not a very efficient way of weeding. As for me, my feet and toes are killing me. And when I try to ignore them, my back starts to ache.

"Kiya-ma! Hello there."

It's the third day after we started weeding. Pretty soon the garden will be finished. I turn at the sound of my name and see Tajima and Sakai, two girls from our class, standing by the wall.

"Oh, uh . . . Hi!"

It's the first time I have seen them since the holidays began. I feel a bit nervous. They are the cutest girls in our class. The boys are split as to who is prettier. Tajima is always tanned. Her eyes are long and almond-shaped, her nose is straight, and her small mouth has a slight pout. She's great at sports. She has a tennis court at her house and says she is happiest when playing tennis with her father. Sakai is always smiling like a TV star. She has pink cheeks and is so pale that the fine downy hairs on her skin shine kind of golden. She looks like a peach fairy. I'm a Tajima fan, Yamashita is a Sakai fan, and Kawabe is neither.

Today they both carry tennis rackets. With their sun visors on, they look more grown-up. They must be going to Tajima's house to play tennis.

"We heard you guys were helping out an old man. That's really nice," Tajima says.

"Mom said we should give you a hand," Sakai says, looking at me and batting her eyes. Even though I prefer Tajima, I can feel myself blushing.

I am about to say, "Sure, come on in," when Kawabe interrupts.

"Sorry, but this is something we decided to do by ourselves. And we'll finish it by ourselves."

The two girls look at each other, surprised and impressed, then give an exclamation as they catch sight of someone at the front door. The old man is standing there with a shopping bag in his hand. When did he go out? We've been so busy weeding we didn't even notice.

Tajima and Sakai stare at him, excited and flustered, as though he were some kind of celebrity. The old man just stands awkwardly in his baggy trousers and sagging gray T-shirt with the shopping bag hanging from his hand. When the two girls say "Hello!" he purses his stubble-covered lips and mumbles, "Hello." It is very different from the way he shouts, "Hey, you!" when he talks to us.

"Did you hear that?" Yamashita hisses, looking at me out of the corner of his eyes. "Girls sure have it good."

"Mmm."

"Good luck with the weeding," the girls call out, and then go on their way.

"You didn't have to chase them away, did you?" I grumble.

"Yeah," Yamashita agrees. "They even offered to help."

"Birdbrain," Kawabe retorts. "I just couldn't stand to see your faces." And he sticks out his tongue.

We attack our work with sudden energy. We stop wasting time chatting to one another and begin pulling weeds just because they are there, forgetting that it is the old man's garden, forgetting cram school, forgetting that it is our last summer holiday before the junior high school entrance exams next year, forgetting our fathers, our mothers, and everything. When we go home, we eat, take a bath, somehow manage to finish our homework, and then collapse into bed. We do not dream, but we have no nightmares, either.

The next evening we finish the job. Now there are only the three of us, the fragrant olive bush, and the clothesline strung in a V still hanging above the dried earth of the garden. No garbage. No weeds. The laundry is folded in a soft pile on the porch. The old man seems to wash his clothes a lot these days.

"We did it!" Yamashita exclaims.

"Sure did!"

"The garden looks so much bigger."

"Like a different place, isn't it?"

"Yeah, really."

We feel great.

The old man brings a big watermelon from inside the house. "Here, cut it," he says. A knife and cutting board have already been laid out. We sit on the porch, as though enticed by the scent of freshly dried laundry and burning mosquito coil.

The old man raps the watermelon with his knuckles and says, "It's perfectly ripe." How could he know

63

that just by tapping it on the outside? Mimicking the old man, Yamashita raps Kawabe's head with his knuckles.

"Ow! What was that for?"

"Just checking."

"You!" Kawabe yells, trying to rap Yamashita's head in return. Yamashita shields his head with his arms and laughs. Kawabe climbs on top of him while Yamashita yells, "Stop! You'll squash me."

"Cut it out, you guys!" I say, and Kawabe raps me on the head.

"What do you think you're doing?"

Yamashita laughs even harder, so I give him a smart smack on the head.

"Ow!"

"What a racket!" The old man looks exasperated. "Go on home."

"We'll go," Kawabe says, "after we eat the watermelon." And he was the one who had told us not to talk to the old man!

"Little brats. Hurry up and eat, then," the old man growls.

Kawabe runs his hand gently over the watermelon. "This is a fruit, right? An enormous fruit. I bet the first person who saw one was pretty surprised."

"Cut it," the old man says to Kawabe.

"I can't."

"Why not?"

"I've never cut one before."

"You've never cut a watermelon?"

"We always buy them already cut. How could we eat a whole one?" Kawabe replies.

"I see," mutters the old man, and looks at the watermelon. It must have been a long time since he himself bought a whole one.

"Why don't you try it, Kawabe?" Yamashita suggests, then looks at the knife and picks it up with a sudden exclamation. "Wait a minute," he says. He stands up as if to leave; then, remembering the knife, lays it carefully on the porch.

"What's up?"

"I'll be right back. Wait for me."

About ten minutes pass before Yamashita returns, panting. He holds something that looks like a long, thin, black stone. When the old man sees it, his eyes widen in admiration. Yamashita grins. I can't figure out what is going on.

"The kitchen sink," the old man says. Yamashita slips off his sneakers, picks up the knife, and walks quickly into the house. I can see him at the kitchen counter silhouetted by the light from a little window in front of it. He wets the long stone-like thing, and then I hear a noise like something scraping and sliding. *Swish-swish, swish-swish.*

"What's he doing?"

The old man takes off his sandals and goes inside. Kawabe and I follow behind him into the small room that serves as the old man's living quarters.

The kotatsu is gone. The only things visible are a little folding table, a TV sitting on a small chest of drawers, a dresser, and the closet. Except for a little blue pillow filled with buckwheat chaff which has been left lying on the thick straw tatami floor mat, the room is neat and tidy. There are no ornaments of any kind. No

65

souvenirs, no artificial flowers faded with dust, not even a calendar advertising beer. It is too empty.

The kitchen beyond the room has a damp, dark smell. The smell of an old house. The cool wooden floorboards stick to the soles of my feet. To the right is the front door, and the toilet and bath are probably to the left. Two pots rest on the shelf hanging above the counter. Just one lonely teacup sits in the washbasin.

Yamashita grips the knife handle firmly in his right hand. The four fingers of his left hand rest neatly on the blade, pushing it regularly back and forth across the stone. His lips are firmly pressed together, his face deep in concentration.

"He's sharpening the knife," Kawabe says in awe.

"He's good, too," says the old man.

"My family runs a fish shop," Yamashita says, resting for a moment. "My dad is much better than me."

Adjusting the knife blade slightly, he begins sharpening again. "The flavor of the fish changes depending on how you cut it," he adds, and then continues silently with his work. I can hear only the swish of the knife and the hum of the cicadas. It is very quiet.

"Are you going to work in the fish store, too?" the old man asks.

"I don't know," Yamashita says, keeping his eyes on the knife, which is starting to shine silver like the back of a fish. He's like a samurai on a TV show sharpening his sword.

"My mom worries that I'll wind up stuck in a little fish shop like my dad. She says nobody will want to marry me, so I should study hard and do something different." The knife stops, and Yamashita turns it around and begins sharpening the other side. "Me, though, I like my dad's job." With that, he runs his thumb over the sharpened edge of the blade as though testing it.

"Whoa! Be careful!" Kawabe says.

"Don't worry." Yamashita laughs. I have never seen him so confident before.

"Have you ever cut yourself?" I ask.

"Sure," he says, as though it was of no consequence. "But if you're too afraid to touch a knife, you'll never learn how to use one."

"Hmm, that's good advice," the old man says.

"My dad told me that," Yamashita says, embarrassed but proud, "when I cut my hand so badly that I was afraid to go near a cutting board. A knife can be used to kill someone, or it can be used to make good food to help someone get better. It's all in how you handle it, my dad says. I already know how to fillet sardines and mackerel."

We are very impressed. Yamashita says, "That should do it," and turns toward the porch. From the cool dampness of the kitchen I can see the summer sun shining on the garden, making it look like a square box made out of sunshine.

The knife slides into the watermelon, and it splits open as though it was waiting for us.

"Mmm. It's ripe and juicy," the old man says.

"This feels good," Kawabe remarks, gazing at the knife as though savoring the feel of his first attempt at cutting watermelon.

The watermelon is so juicy it looks as though legions of the black seed soldiers nestled in the red flesh will come leaping out. We cut the watermelon in half, the half into quarters, and each quarter in half again. Then we dig in. It is delicious, especially since we are so thirsty. The old man cuts his piece in half again and takes small bites, chewing carefully.

"Is it good?" he asks us.

"Mmmmmm."

"Ah! Nothing like watermelon after a good day's work," Yamashita says, his eyes half closed.

Kawabe takes off his shirt. "Watermelon juice stains," he says.

Yamashita and I strip to the waist, too. We haven't been swimming yet this summer and our stomachs are white like a frog's belly. You can see the marks of our T-shirt sleeves on our arms.

"Must be weeder's tan," I say, and the old man laughs loudly, not his usual short snort of a laugh.

"Look at you two. If I added you together and then divided by two, you'd be just right," Kawabe says, looking at Yamashita and then at me, all skin and bones.

"Thanks, but we don't need your criticism," I say.

"Yeah, that's right," Yamashita agrees.

Kawabe isn't as skinny as I am, but his skin is kind of transparent, like a fish's, and he looks like a real weakling. He doesn't seem to have grown any taller since Yamashita outdistanced him recently, either. Stripped to the waist as he is, the glasses perched on his thin nose look very heavy.

"Why don't you take your glasses off?" I say.

"What for?" Kawabe asks as he takes a bite of watermelon. The bones stand out clearly on his rounded back.

"Heck, I don't know," I say, feeling a bit irritable.

"What day is it tomorrow?" Kawabe asks suddenly.

"Wednesday," the old man answers.

"A garbage day," Kawabe says, holding the watermelon rind between his fingers.

"Uh-oh." Yamashita looks up at the sky. "Rain."

Dark stains appear on the dry whitened earth, spreading across the entire garden. The sound of heavy raindrops fills our ears. The smells of damp earth and mosquito coil rise strongly.

"We should plant some seeds in the fall." The old man's voice reaches my ears as though weaving through the rain. "Marigolds or something like that."

"Why wait till fall? Let's plant them tomorrow." Once he gets an idea into his head, Kawabe just can't wait.

"You sure are impatient." The old man gives Kawabe a sidelong look.

"I don't think you're supposed to plant seeds in summer," Yamashita says.

"Who cares? They can wait in the soil till it's time to come up."

"Yeah, why not? Let's plant them tomorrow," I say. Yamashita still looks unconvinced.

"What do you think we should plant, Yamashita?" I ask.

"Ummm—"

"Lenten rose," the old man interrupts.

"Narcissus," Kawabe chimes in.

"Violets," I say.

"Daikon radish," says Yamashita.

"Daikon radish!? What do you mean daikon radish?" Kawabe snorts in disgust.

"They have flowers, too," Yamashita says indignantly.

"That's right," says the old man. "White flowers like rape-seed blossoms."

"Really? I didn't know that."

"Afternoon lady," I say.

"Wild pink," Kawabe says.

"Asters," Yamashita says.

"Amaryllis," the old man says.

Anemone, dogtooth violet, butterbur, peony, orange stonecrop, campanula . . .

The old man lists flowers that we have never heard of before. Listening to his voice, we imagine fields full of flowers and watch the rain fall into the empty garden. We tune our ears to the sound of the heavens watering the earth, the earth that waits to be reborn as new life takes root.

IKEDA SEED STORE, the sign says in peeling paint. When cram school finished, we went directly to the old wooden two-story house which sits wedged between two buildings near the train station. The sliding glass door is open, but it is very dark inside.

"Maybe we should try the flower shop beside the station," Kawabe says, peering inside. He's talking about a new store, recently built, with white tile siding.

"No way," I insist. "This is a specialty store." I have been here once before, to buy morning-glory seeds when I was in first grade. My mother brought me because I lost the seeds the teacher had given me for a project. I planted the seeds we bought and watered them every day. The vines grew taller than the bamboo poles I had put in the planter, curling around the veranda posts, up the screen door, and, when there was nowhere left to go, stretching out like thin hands in supplication to the sky until they suddenly broke. They bore many big flowers which bloomed one after the other. When we compared our observation diaries at school, I found that my plant had borne more flowers than anybody else's. My mother and I made colored water with the petals and dyed I don't know how many white handkerchiefs. Come to think of it, my mother didn't drink back then.

Now I suddenly recall that we were supposed to collect the seeds when the flowers withered as part of the project. I had collected the seeds one by one, even the ones I dropped, and put them in an envelope. Red, white, and purple flowers lay sleeping in those shiny black seeds. I wonder where that envelope went?

"Hello?"

The store is cool inside. It is filled with little drawers. There is a musty old-house smell of cooking and incense.

"Yes, yes." A dark-blue curtain divides the store from the rest of the house. The sound of footsteps moving across tatami floor mats comes nearer, and the curtain parts for an instant, allowing a sudden shaft of bright light into the room. At the same moment a wind chime sounds on the other side of the curtain.

A little old woman appears. Her small arms sticking out of the half-sleeves of her mauve blouse are slightly bent, as though in hesitation. Small hands. Small mouth. Small round eyes. Her white hair is bound in a bun at the back of her head. She is shorter than I am. She wears tiny sandals and ankle socks on her dainty feet. She looks like a little girl.

"We want to buy some seeds."

"Yes. What kind would you like?"

"Are there any that are good for planting at this time of year?"

"We're going to plant them today," Kawabe adds.

"It's already August," she says, and thinks a moment. "If I had some Lenten rose it would be good."

"Hey! That's one the old man mentioned yesterday," Yamashita exclaims.

"That's right!"

"Give us some of those."

"They are planted in summer, but I don't have any here because people don't usually plant them from seeds," the old woman says regretfully.

She begins to open each drawer slowly and carefully, closing one before going on to the next, saying to herself, "Something to plant *now*." Each drawer is filled with little packages of seeds neatly lined up like rows of book cards in a library file. In each dark drawer, a garden sleeps, waiting for water and light. I almost expect my little envelope of morning-glory seeds to appear.

The old woman moves with tidy little steps and turns to face us. "Are you going to plant them in a planter?" she asks. I wonder if I met her the last time I came here.

"A garden."

"A flower bed, then."

"No. We're going to scatter them over the whole yard. All at once," Kawabe says.

"Ah, I see." The old woman smiles.

Once again she moves methodically toward the drawers. "Then this should be just the thing," she says, taking a packet from a drawer and turning primly toward me. She places it politely in my hands. It is a packet of cosmos seeds. The instructions say to plant by mid-June.

"If you plant them now, they won't grow very tall, but they will bloom. I'm sure these will grow nicely if you scatter them all over the yard," she says, "because cosmos grow only in wide-open spaces." She also tells us that we won't need to use fertilizer at this time of year but can just scatter them.

"How many would you like?"

"Hmmm . . ."

"If you're going to scatter them over the whole yard, you'll need ten or twenty packets." The old woman really seems to like the idea of scattering them.

"How much are they?" Yamashita asks. Until then I haven't even thought about money.

"One hundred yen per packet."

We turn away from the old woman and consult. "How much money do you have?"

"Four hundred," Kawabe says.

"Three hundred and fifty. It's my lunch money," says Yamashita.

I have three hundred. That makes a total of 1,050 yen among the three of us.

"Okay. Let's buy as many as we can with this amount."

"What about my lunch?" Yamashita asks.

"Skip it."

"Huh?"

"It won't kill you to skip a meal," Kawabe says, and Yamashita falls silent.

When we turn around, the old woman is already deftly putting packets of seeds into a paper bag.

"Grandma," a voice calls from behind the curtain, and a girl about high-school age pokes her head out.

"Oh, you have customers." Her long hair is tied back and her slightly pointed chin and rounded forehead are just like the old woman's.

"Elly, give me a hand, would you?"

"Sure." The girl's white blouse seems to flutter through the darkened shop as she helps her grandmother collect all the cosmos packets from the drawer and put them in the bag.

"They're going to scatter the seeds over the whole yard."

"Well, in that case, cosmos are just perfect. And they don't take much looking after." She looks at Kawabe and smiles. "You're lucky you have a garden."

"It's the old man's," Kawabe says, looking down at his feet suddenly. "I live in an apartment." His voice almost fades away. He is jiggling again. I grip his shoulder.

The girl looks at Kawabe for a minute and then says gently, "I see." She falls silent, working swiftly.

"Here you are." The bag is stuffed full.

"But—"

"It's all right. Take them all. They're leftover stock from spring," the old woman says. "Besides, this shop will be closing soon." She laughs, a sad little laugh, then says, "It's wonderful that you're planting a garden when you're so young." She bows politely.

"Your grandfather will be very glad." The girl nods in approval.

The old woman says we don't need to pay, but we place our 1,050 yen on the counter anyway and take the package, saying "Thanks!" From that moment until we plant the seeds, Kawabe cradles the bag carefully and doesn't utter a word even when spoken to.

We open all the packets and find that we have a heaping bowlful of seeds. Long, dry, slender seeds. We take a handful of them, bend down, and, rather than scattering them, plant them carefully in the ground.

"So many?" the old man asks in surprise. "How come?"

"We held up the seed store," I answer.

"As if you were capable of armed robbery!" the old man snorts. He was the one who had accused us of being thieves in the first place. I guess he has forgotten.

"Seems strange to go to all the trouble of planting cosmos," he remarks. "In the country, they grow like weeds."

"The country?"

"Hokkaido."

"Oh?"

"Yes, it was back when I was about your age." He closes his eyes for a moment. I close mine, too. I can hear the rustling sound of the wind blowing through a field of cosmos in full bloom. I wonder what the old man looked like when he was a kid. He couldn't have been balding then. He was probably thin and maybe darkly tanned. I try hard to imagine it. But no matter how I try, it is myself I see standing in the field.

"Do you know the meaning of cosmos flowers?" Yamashita asks.

"No."

"A . . . something or other . . . maiden."

"What do you mean, 'something or other'?"

"It's on the back of the packet. A something or other maiden."

There are more than fifty seed packets scattered on the porch, each with a picture of cosmos flowers on the front. It looks like the cosmos have already bloomed there on the porch. I take one of the packets and look at the back. Japanese name: akizakura, daishungiku. Family: chrysanthemum. Product of Mexico. Meaning: an immaculate maiden.

"What does it say?" Yamashita asks. But it seems like a word I shouldn't say.

"See. You can't read it either, Kiyama."

"I can, too."

"Then what does it say?"

"Immaculate," I say loudly, irritated. "Yamashita, can't you even read 'immaculate'?"

Yamashita straightens up and turns toward me. "What does it mean?"

No wonder his grades for language class are so bad. "It means 'not dirty.' "

"Not dirty?"

"Like not having done anything bad," I mutter.

"What kind of bad thing, I wonder," Yamashita says absently. "Like playing hooky or eating snacks in the middle of the night, maybe."

"I don't know."

"Or like not showing your parents your report card. Lying isn't good, either."

The old man chuckles.

"Quit gabbing and get to work!" Kawabe says in annoyance.

"What's up, Kawabe?" Yamashita asks. "You've been so quiet since the store."

"Leave him alone," I say. I don't tell him that Kawabe is thinking about the girl in the store. It wouldn't be right.

The old man fetches an ancient hose from the house. The spout is tied on with string. Saying "Shh!" he jerks his head toward Kawabe, who has his back turned to us. Yamashita suppresses a wicked chuckle, slips off his sneakers, and goes into the kitchen to turn on the tap where the hose is connected.

"Okay!" he whispers. I aim carefully. The next moment, water comes shooting out.

"Hey! That's cold!" Kawabe whirls about to face us. "Cut it out!"

He runs about the garden, trying to escape. I work the hose so that he won't stomp on the newly planted seeds. It looks like he's dancing. Yamashita and I, and the old man, too, are killing ourselves laughing.

"Wow! That's beautiful." We hear girls talking on the other side of the wall. It is Tajima and Sakai. Kawabe stops in surprise and the water hits him square on the butt.

"A rainbow. It's really pretty," Tajima says.

"Hey. She's right." By changing the angle of the hose, we can see a little rainbow from the porch. The seven colors of sunlight. Usually they are invisible, but now they reveal themselves within a single stream of water. Even though the light was always there, the colors had remained hidden. There must be millions of things like that in the world. They exist, but they are hidden, so we can't see them. Some of them reveal themselves because of some simple change, while others are only discovered after a long, difficult search by scientists or explorers. I wonder if there is something hidden now that is waiting for me to discover it.

At that moment, the nozzle which was tied to the hose suddenly flies off. The water gushes out, making a small hole in the ground where we planted the seeds.

"Ah!" The old man hurriedly grabs the hose from me and squeezes the end, trying to control the flow of water. It arches in a straight line, hitting the stunned Kawabe right in the face.

"Wa-blurb!" he splutters. The girls' laughter rises in the air like birds in flight.

"Whoops! Sorry about that. You all right?" the old man says, suppressing a laugh. Yamashita suddenly comes to his senses and runs in to turn off the tap.

I count my breaths when I lie in bed. One, two, three, four, five, six . . . fourteen, fifteen, sixteen, seventeen . . . After thirty I start to fall asleep. Sleep wraps itself around me and pulls me under, but sometimes I float back to the surface like an old shoe in water and I start counting again from the beginning. One, two, three, four . . .

A long time ago I read that in one lifetime a person breathes from six hundred million to eight hundred million times, and I couldn't stop trying to count my breaths all day. It was in second grade, I think. But as I'd count, I wouldn't be able to keep breathing. When the lack of air became unbearable, I would burst out coughing and have to start counting all over again. I counted during class and even while I was eating. I'd gasp and cough so often that my mother would get irritated and say, "Stop that coughing!" But I didn't know how.

In my bed at night I would cry and scream, "I can't breathe! I've forgotten how! I'm going to die! Mom!" At first my mother would sit by my pillow or bring me warm milk to drink. This would calm me for a while, but as soon as she left I would be overcome by the same fear. "I can't breathe! I'm going to die!"

I don't need to call my mother anymore, but I still count my breaths before I go to sleep. How many times have I breathed since I was born? If we breathe eight hundred million times in eighty years, then at twelve I must have breathed 120 million times. One hundred and twenty million little puffs of air have passed through my lungs. How many more times will this go on? Someday it will just stop, as though suddenly cut off. At five, eight, nine hundred million times, or maybe at only three hundred million times. And then . . . where will I go? Or maybe there is no place to go.

I try to stop breathing. I shove my face in my pillow and count. One, two, three . . . thirteen, fourteen, fifteen, sixteen . . . thirty, thirty-one, thirty-two, thirty-three, thirty-four . . . I close my eyes tightly. Yellow lights flicker in the darkness, becoming a field of yellow flowers. My body starts to float as though I am a bird looking down on the field. No, a fire. The yellow flowers become little flames rising higher and spreading around me, forming a sea of flame. Someone stands there. Their feet are covered in flame and they wave to me. Who is it? But there it ends. I cannot stand it any longer and my whole body gasps for air.

My uncle told me a long, long time ago when I was little that dying means to stop breathing. And for a long time I believed it. But now I know that that's not true. Living is more than just breathing. So dying must be more, too.

The next day we begin to fix the old man's house. We nail the siding back onto the outer wall and get a repairman to replace the broken glass. We sand the window frame, which is split from too much sun, and coat it with paint we bought from the hardware store. Yamashita brings a wooden crate that held salmon from his parents' shop, breaks it apart, and uses the slats to fix the holes in the storm window case.

The old man shows us how to use a file, how to thin paint, how to paint, how to saw. We bang our thumbs with the hammer, knock the paint over, and struggle to extract the saw from the boards when we make a crooked cut.

Sugita and Matsushita come to spy on us as usual.

"Hey!" I call from the top of the ladder. "Could you pass me that can of paint? I left it at the bottom."

Kawabe is busy trying to fit the newly painted window back into its frame, and Yamashita is patching a tear in a screen window, gripping a needle with his thick fingers. I wave my brush at Matsushita.

Matsushita looks at Sugita, wondering what he should do. Sugita glances at the can of beige paint and then looks at me suspiciously. "What about soccer?" he says.

"What?"

"Are you coming or not?"

Then I remember. Today is the first soccer practice since the summer holidays started. "I forgot."

"Well, what are you going to do?" Sugita persists. I wish he would just leave me alone.

"We're a bit busy here today. Tell the coach I won't be coming."

Matsushita's eyes widen.

"What about those guys?" Sugita asks, pointing his chin toward Kawabe and Yamashita.

"Hey!" I yell so Kawabe and Yamashita can hear. "There's soccer practice today. Are you going?"

"No way. I can't just drop this in the middle." Even though he's good at soccer, Kawabe doesn't seem inclined to go.

"Oh, sorry. I forgot. Mom didn't say anything about it," Yamashita says without the least trace of regret in his voice.

"Well, I guess that's it, then. So hurry up and pass me the paint can, will you?" I say to Sugita. He backs away from me and then suddenly takes off at a run, with Matsushita following behind. Cowards. Those guys really are cowards.

"Here." The old man passes me the paint can. I start painting the wooden fence beige. My back is turned to him, but I know the old man is watching me. The old man often watches us when he thinks we aren't looking. Once I forgot a book called *Scarecrow* on the porch. It was a really scary story about an English kid our age. The old man returned it to me without even having to ask whose it was.

In the beginning, we had watched the old man, but now it turns out that he is watching us. But it's different from the way my mom stares at me while she drinks and I eat my dinner.

The paint job looks pretty uneven, but the house seems to have been reborn. Sitting in the shade of the fragrant olive bush, we examine the results of our labors one by one. The beige fence, the green window frames and door. Even the storm doors have been painted green. From here, the blue corrugated tin roof doesn't look so bad. Any stranger who saw the house now would want to come up and knock on the door.

"When the cosmos bloom it'll be just like in *Little House on the Prairie*," Yamashita says. All over the yard cosmos are beginning to sprout amid the weeds that are poking their heads up again. I offer to pull up the weeds, but the old man says not yet, they just started.

He crosses his arms and looks thoughtful. "It doesn't seem like the same house," he says.

"You're not kidding. Before it didn't even look like someone was living here," says Kawabe. The old man gives him a sideways glance, but Kawabe doesn't even notice. He is too busy gazing proudly at the storm doors, the green paint drying in gobs and streaks.

"Yes," the old man says, looking once more at the transformed house. "You're right. It's been a long time since I took care of the place."

"It's worth it, isn't it?" I say.

"Yep. It is worth it." He nods emphatically, as

though at this old age he has just realized it for the first time.

"Have you ever been married?" Kawabe asks.

"Yes," he answers, as though talking about someone else.

"What happened to her? Did she die?"

"Uh, no."

"You split up?"

"Yes, I guess you might say that."

"Why?"

"I forget."

"Didn't you marry again?"

"Nope."

"Why?"

"I don't know." The old man seems uninterested.

"What was her name?"

"I forget."

"Did you have kids?"

"Nope."

"That's weird."

"How's that?"

"My dad married twice, and had kids with both."

"So? Sounds all right to me." The old man gives a little sigh.

"It's not all right!" Kawabe falls silent, thinking about something. "Maybe if you had had kids, my dad wouldn't have remarried."

"That's nonsense!"

"Well, don't you think it could be so?"

"Why is it my fault that your father married twice?"

"Not your fault. But maybe the world is just set up like that."

"I don't get it."

"Well, I don't get it, either," Kawabe says a little angrily. "I don't understand anything, so I think that maybe there's some kind of hidden rule somewhere." He is silent for a while. Then suddenly he raises his head and begins talking loudly and rapidly. "For instance, if A has one apple and B has two apples, how many apples are there all together? Three. Very good. But it's not as simple as that. And that's what I don't understand. You see what I mean? I can't split my dad in two, and even though I have no father at home now, and you are on your own, you can't be my father, either. Because we're not apples. But there must be some way for things to work out better, and that's what I'm looking for. People have discovered the great laws of nature, haven't they? Like the fact that the earth is surrounded by atmosphere, and that birds have wings and can fly through the sky. That's why we were able to invent the airplane, right? So tell me, if there are planes that fly faster than the speed of sound, why don't I have a father in my house? And why does my mother look so worried when she goes shopping on Sundays? And why does she have to keep telling me to make my father regret it someday?"

He breaks off his torrent of words and says, simply, "Let's go home."

The old man strides across the garden heedless of the newly sprouting cosmos, enters the house, and brings out a knife and a watermelon. He cuts the watermelon into four pieces and says, "Here. Eat before you go."

"No thanks." Kawabe looks at his feet, as though feeling awkward.

85

"Come on."

Kawabe eats. First one tentative bite; then, burying his whole face in the enormous chunk of watermelon, he chomps away furiously. We all dig into the sweet juicy flesh of the sun-ripened watermelon as though attacking some unknown enemy.

8

The old man doesn't let his garbage pile up anymore. He wakes early and takes it to the collection site by the telephone pole himself. When he meets us on the street, he greets us heartily. We mumble, "Good morning." When cram school finishes for the day, we take a peek into the garden from the fence. Even the tallest cosmos are only about five inches high, with thin green leaves. Although the old woman at the seed store warned us that they wouldn't grow very tall, they still look puny.

"Do you think they'll really bloom? I hope they're all right," one of us always says.

"Yeah, me, too," another agrees.

Sometimes the window is open. Perhaps the old man is on the other side of the screen ironing his clothes in the tatami room, where the breeze can reach him. He doesn't watch TV so much anymore.

After checking on the flowers, each of us goes his own way home or we might go together to the school swimming pool. Kawabe no longer suggests that we spy on the old man. The old man goes shopping, cooks for himself, eats properly, cleans, and does his laundry. It seems like there is nothing more for us to do.

"I've got to study," Kawabe says, sitting on the side of the pool after swimming for a while. The heat of the sun soaks into our backs and makes my nose feel tingly, as if I am about to cry.

"I really bombed that last test. My mom threw a fit. She locked me out of the apartment."

"Really?"

Kawabe gazes despondently at the pool. Yamashita is doing a sluggish backstroke. He is almost entirely submerged in water.

"I was locked out so long that the lady who lives next door came over in the middle of the night and my mom finally let me in."

I didn't do well on the summer midterm tests, either. The cram school even phoned my mother.

"What have you been doing every day?" My mother gave me a dirty look.

"What do you mean?" My mom still had the same look on her face. There was no need to look at me like that just for getting bad grades once. She doesn't trust me at all. "I'll study harder . . ."

"Maybe I should have put you in a cram school where none of your school friends go," my mom said, as though she hadn't even heard me.

"That's got nothing to do with it." I went to my

room. I started studying, but just couldn't seem to concentrate.

"Hey!" Kawabe is looking around the pool. "Where's Yamashita?"

Maybe he got out, I think. But we are the only ones who aren't in the water. "I wonder where he could be," I say.

"Look! Over there!" Kawabe points at the far end of the pool.

"Huh?"

Suddenly a shrill whistle blows and a teacher jumps into the pool. It's our phys. ed. instructor, Miss Kondo. We can see her blue-and-green-striped bathing suit shoot through the water, and then she is lifting something limp and heavy from the bottom of the pool.

Yamashita!

Everyone gathers at the edge of the pool. Yamashita is lying inert, his eyes lightly closed. His face and body are very pale.

"Is he dead?" someone asks. The teacher does not respond, but presses firmly on Yamashita's chest, releases, then presses again. Her bangs have escaped from her swimming cap and are plastered against her pale forehead and down the bridge of her nose. Yamashita doesn't move.

"Yamashita! Yamashita!" the teacher calls, slapping him on the cheek.

"Uh-oh! He's going to die," Sugita says from behind me.

"Shut up!" I yell, surprising even myself by the shrillness of my voice. Kawabe is waggling his chin and jiggling.

The teacher pinches Yamashita's nose between her

89

fingers and, placing her lips on his mouth, blows. Five times, six times, seven times . . . Everyone is very still.

I remember Yamashita's hands when he sharpened the knife. His face when he laughs, his little eyes seeming to disappear. His body soaked with sweat when he runs, always at the end of the line. His voice when he welcomes customers to the fish store wearing his apron. I realize for the first time that to die meant all of those things would disappear from before my eyes; it meant that I would never see him again. Never again? Never see Yamashita even one more time? Would the world still go on as though nothing happened, as though it was still summer and I was still alive? The thought terrifies me.

"Yamashita, you old fatso! Snap out of it!" I yell.

A faint blush rises to his cheeks, his eyelids flicker, and Yamashita slowly opens his eyes.

"What . . . what's the matter with all of you?" he asks.

We wait for Yamashita while he rests in the nurse's room and then walk him home. The teacher offers to call his mother, but Yamashita insists that she do no such thing. We stop in the middle of the pedestrian bridge over the railway tracks and look down absently at the trains passing beneath us. It is the same bridge from which Kawabe once considered jumping.

"Lucky you! You got to kiss Miss Kondo," Kawabe says, drawing his eyebrows together and looking at Yamashita. Yamashita squirms. Miss Kondo is beautiful. Long eyelashes; bright, clear eyes; and a sculpted mouth. She looks a bit like a movie star.

"Yeah, you lucky devil," I say.

"So how was it, anyway?" Kawabe asks.

"How would I know? I was unconscious, remember?" Yamashita protests.

"Not that, stupid. I was asking about"—Kawabe brings his face right up to Yamashita's—"when you were unconscious. We thought you were going to die, you know."

Yamashita looks completely baffled.

"So what is it like to almost die?"

Yamashita opens his mouth as if to say something and then closes it, lost in thought.

"I remember getting a cramp in my leg," he says, after some time. "But after that, there's nothing."

"You mean you don't remember?"

"Uh-uh."

"Not even if it hurt or anything?"

"No. Nothing." Yamashita looks rather apologetic. "But I did have a dream."

"What kind of dream?" Kawabe and I both lean forward eagerly.

"I was in the ocean. Riding on the back of a flounder. A school of sardines was swimming nearby, shining silver. It was beautiful." He raises his round chin and gazes upward.

Maybe the next world is on the bottom of the sea. Deep down at the unknown bottom.

"The flounder could talk. He said, 'The princess of the sea is ill. She must eat flounder sashimi in order to get better. O great hero, you will make me into sashimi, won't you?' "

"And then?"

"I didn't think I would be able to cut up a talking fish. And besides, I don't know how to make sashimi from flounder yet. So I said that I had to go back. That I would come back another time. And then . . ."

"And then?"

"I woke up."

"Hmmm."

I wonder if Yamashita will remember this dream when he becomes an expert at making flounder into sashimi.

"Lucky you could come back," Kawabe says, as if to himself.

"Yeah," Yamashita says, and shivers. A train passes under the bridge with a roar.

"Maybe dying is pretty simple, after all. Don't you think?" Kawabe asks me. "You could die in a car accident, or be hit on the head as you pass by a construction site. Or drown in a pool."

"Or fall and crack your head," I say. "Or be struck down by a stray bullet from a gang war."

"Or be poisoned when eating blowfish," Yamashita says.

"I am never going to eat blowfish, ever," Kawabe says emphatically. "But you know, I think it is probably more amazing that we are alive."

I remember a slide we saw in science class of a butterfly laying eggs. Insects lay hundreds of eggs. But sometimes not even one grows into a butterfly. Almost all of them are eaten by other bugs, or they die because they can't find enough leaves to eat or because of bad weather. It's almost as if they are born to die.

"I guess dying isn't so strange. After all, everyone dies," I say, and Kawabe nods in agreement.

"But I'm still afraid to die. Aren't you?"

"Yeah."

"That's weird. If everyone dies, anyway, why is death so scary? I guess we won't know until we die."

"You know," Yamashita says slowly, "I can't make flounder into sashimi yet. And I don't want to die until I know how. If I think about dying before I've learned, I feel afraid. But I don't know whether I will be content to die even once I have learned."

Will I ever master something so well that I feel ready to die? Even if I don't master it completely, I want to find something like that. Because if I don't, then why am I alive?

The second week of August, a typhoon strikes the city. The wind screams above our insignificant little town, racing through the streets. Every time its great voice pauses to draw a breath, the rain pelts our window.

The buses aren't running, so cram school is canceled. I press my face against the living-room window and watch the outside world being devoured by the enormous monster. Even in midday, the streets are dyed dark gray within the monster's belly. There is not a soul in sight. A small sign flies through the air like a snowmobile whizzing along an invisible slope.

"Mom."

My mother is sitting on the couch, dozing.

"Mother!" She looks too pale. As if she is very tired. Maybe it's because her shoulder-length hair has fallen across her face, half hiding it. Last night I woke to the sound of her voice yelling. I listened and heard my father saying something in a hoarse whisper in the bedroom next door. After that I didn't hear my mother's voice anymore.

I put my ear near my mother's mouth. One, two, three, four . . . I feel her warm, moist breath on my ear. The tiny wind that blows through my mother's body passes into my ear and vibrates in my brain.

The room is very quiet. The aluminum sash windows are shut tight, and the air conditioner has chilled the room. In a room like this, you could sleep right through the end of the world as if it did not matter at all. This must be what the inside of a tomb is like. The dead lying beneath the cold earth listening to the distant voices from the bustling world above . . .

I get up quietly so as not to wake my mother, and open the outside door. The storm swallows me and I run as though the wind will steal me away.

Just as I thought: The old man's garden is a giant puddle. Only the weeds are still standing. The cosmos lie flattened in the water. They may never recover.

The rain stings my eyes and I stand for a while by the fence, squinting into the garden. I didn't bring an umbrella. Even if I had, it would be of no use.

"What are you doing? Get inside!" The front door opens a crack and I can see half the old man's face. He must be forcing the door open against the wind. He is gritting his teeth. "Hurry up!"

I run in and the door slams behind me. The moaning of the wind recedes. As I stand in the hall drying my hair with a towel the old man hands me, my eyes catch sight of two familiar pairs of sneakers sitting beside the door.

"Hi!" Yamashita sticks his head out from the tatami room.

Kawabe bounces out of the kitchen. "Take your socks off," he orders.

I take off my sodden socks and wipe myself, shirt and shorts and all, with the towel. The towel becomes damp and heavy. Then I step inside.

"Here. Give me those." Kawabe takes the towel and my socks and carries them promptly to the bathtub.

"I was looking out the window on the second floor of our house and I saw someone walking along with an umbrella turned inside out. And who should it be but Kawabe." Yamashita does a little imitation of Kawabe battling against the wind, holding an imaginary pair of glasses on his nose with one hand. "He said he was going to make sure the cosmos were all right, so I came along. You, too?"

"Yeah." I'm a little annoyed that they beat me to it.

"I washed your socks for you," Kawabe says, coming back from the bathtub. He sits down as if he owns the place.

"Well, sit down," the old man says to me. He is sitting perfectly relaxed in his usual spot by the window. I sit in one corner, feeling a little awkward.

"So what were you doing?" I ask.

"Nothing." The two look at each other.

"Nothing? Hah! Not you two!" The old man is in a good humor.

"Well, what were you doing, then?" I ask. Kawabe and Yamashita grin sheepishly.

"Never mind. If you don't feel like telling me." The jerks. Trying to leave me out.

"We were betting. Whether you would come or not," Yamashita says.

"Me?"

"Yup."

"Is that all?" Was that all?

"Well, no; it's not, not for us, anyway." Kawabe and Yamashita are pouting.

"So who won?"

The old man points to himself. "All right, you two. You owe me a massage."

Yamashita massages his shoulders, Kawabe his left foot, and for some reason I wind up massaging his right foot.

"Why do I have to do this? It was you guys who lost."

"Stop complaining. It was your fault that we lost," Kawabe retorts.

"That's ridiculous!"

Yamashita sits on the old man's back and grunts as he works his stubby fingers into the muscles on his shoulders. "I'm pretty good, aren't I?"

"Ergh," the old man groans. He lies on his stomach with his eyes closed and a grimace on his face.

"I often massage my dad's shoulders. I'm used to it."

"Ergh."

"My dad's shoulders are about three times as thick as yours."

"Arghh."

"Feels good, huh?"

"Arghhhhh."

"Maybe I should massage a little harder."

"Errraghhhhh."

"Don't be afraid to ask."

"I—it hurts!"

"Oh!" Yamashita lets go of his shoulders. "You should have told me sooner!"

The old man gasps for breath.

I roll his slacks up to his knees. His calves are very thin. The scanty skin and flesh move slowly in my hand as if they do not want to have anything to do with the hard bone. My father's legs are covered in thick hair, but the old man's leg is smooth like oiled paper, yet all loose and flabby when I touch it. It feels really weird.

"Hey, right leg," the old man says, still lying face down.

"Who me?"

"I bet you've never massaged anyone before, right?"

"Yeah."

"I can tell."

Geez! Up until then I was trying to be very careful, but now I am mad and squeeze really hard.

"Don't take it so seriously! . . . That's more like it. You, turn on the TV."

He has some nerve. I stand up, turn on the TV, and go back to massaging his legs.

A newscaster is saying that war has broken out in some faraway country. A shot of an airport at night with warplanes lined up ready for takeoff flashes on the TV screen. Helmeted pilots climb into the cockpits. The airplanes look like great birds languidly spreading their wings amid the bustle of mechanics and men holding flags on the ground. The pilots wave proudly. Like in a movie.

"Have you ever been to war?" I ask.

The old man, who was watching the TV with his head resting on his folded arms, gives me a quick glance. Then he stares back at the TV.

"Yes."

"Did you fly in a plane?"

"No."

"What did you do?"

"Well, it was a war, you know," he says without taking his eyes off the television. The screen shows a town reduced to rubble.

"Tell us. Tell us about the war. What did you do?" Kawabe's hands keep on massaging, but his eyes are flashing.

"I walked around in the jungle."

"You just walked?" Kawabe is disappointed. "Come on, tell us. Tell us more."

The old man sits up without a word and switches the TV off with a snap. The sound of the rain seems suddenly louder. A wind chime has been left out somewhere and is ringing wildly.

"Come on!" Kawabe rocks back and forth as though he can't contain himself.

"I forget," the old man says without budging.

"That's not fair!" Kawabe protests.

"You can't leave well enough alone, can you?"

"Tell us," I say. "What is war like? We want to know."

The old man thinks awhile. "It's a frightening story," he says, and then falls silent once again. He is sitting cross-legged and his right knee begins to tremble. He looks at us out of the corner of his eyes, then closes them.

It really is frightening.

The old man's troop had retreated from the front line and prowled around the jungle. In other words, they deserted. There were twenty-five of them to start with, but little by little their numbers dwindled to eighteen. They died of heat exhaustion, starvation, and thirst, or were left behind when they fell ill. Occasionally they came across a member of another troop that had been left behind like that. Maggots squirmed in their eyes and mouths even though they were still breathing. Nobody tried to help them. They would all die in the end, anyway. The men in his troop chewed a bitter plant to try to alleviate their hunger and kept on walking because they were afraid of stopping. That's what the old man told us.

When night fell, they cowered like chickens on top of the twisted, sticky tree roots and tried to sleep. There was no room to lie down in the jungle. Some became so exhausted that they didn't care anymore if they lived or died. They just wanted to stretch out and sleep, so they went to the seashore and were riddled with bullets by the enemy . . .

"You're lucky you came out alive!" Yamashita exclaims.

The old man falls silent. He stares absently at Yamashita as if he were a complete stranger.

"Then one day," he continues, "one day we found a small village. A little village with a few huts, their roofs thatched with woven grass. I was so relieved. Now we would have enough food and fresh water to last many days. If we had not found that village then, I think we all would have died."

The wind must have changed direction, for the rain is beating fiercely at the window. Like some creature which has come from far away screaming, "Let me in!"

"But there was something we had to do first."

We sit silently waiting for the old man to continue.

"There were only women, children, and the elderly in the village. We killed them all. The women, the children, the old people."

"Why?" I ask without thinking.

"If we had let them live, they might have told the enemy where we were. Then we would have been killed."

"Rat-a-tat-tat! With a machine gun or something?" Kawabe asks. He is jiggling again.

"Yes," the old man answers flatly.

"What's it feel like to kill someone?" Kawabe's eyes are very bright. Yamashita pokes him, trying to get him to shut up.

"One woman escaped. I ran after her. I was weak from starvation and my legs cramped and I could hardly breathe when I ran. She was young, fast as a doe. Her long ponytail danced on her back, and the muscles on her legs moved powerfully with each step. I fixed my eyes on them and chased her for my life through the jungle. My head was ringing 'bong, bong,' like there was a gong inside it, and still I chased her, though I did not know anymore who I was chasing or why, and I shot her with my gun. She fell like a big sack of flour."

No one speaks. I feel like I can hear a gong ringing. Or maybe it's the groaning of the wind.

"The bullet passed through her back and out her chest on the other side. I went closer. She lay face down, so I turned her over carefully. That was when I noticed." The old man stops for a moment. "She was with child."

"You mean she was pregnant?" Yamashita asks in a small voice. The old man nods.

"I touched her swollen belly with the palm of my hand, and something moved beneath the smooth skin stretched so tight it seemed it would burst. Even though its mother was already dead."

The old man is looking down and I cannot see his face.

"I went back to the village and ate up the food with my mates. And that is how I survived."

He finishes his story and then adds lamely, "It was war, you know." Kawabe is still jiggling slightly. Yamashita sits with his mouth half open, staring fixedly at a handle on the dresser.

We remain quiet for a long time. The old man takes out a cigarette from a drawer on the TV stand and, using a match from the mosquito-coil tray, lights up. It's the first time I have seen the old man smoke. He takes a little puff, then stares at the lighted tip of the cigarette and grinds it out in the tray.

"I bet you wish you had never heard that story."

"Well, no," I mumble, but it just seems to make the feeling in the room even worse.

"Well, why shouldn't you talk about it?" Kawabe says abruptly. "That kind of thing, it's better for you to talk about it. I'm sure it is."

The old man looks a little taken aback. "I see," he says, and looks out the window. The rain has slackened a bit, but continues to fall in sudden spurts and hiccups like a crying baby just before it falls asleep.

"That must be why the old man left his wife," Kawabe declares.

It had not occurred to me or Yamashita until he said it, but it made sense. The old man killed a woman on an island in the South Seas. A woman carrying a child within her belly. To escape from that memory, he ran away from everything, from his home, his wife, his own happiness.

"But there must be lots of other people who did the same kind of thing," Yamashita says. He thinks a minute and then adds, "What if that woman becomes a ghost? She'll haunt the old man, holding a baby in her arms."

102   "Knock it off!" Kawabe glares at Yamashita.

"War stinks," I say. Kawabe looks down and nods.

The day of the typhoon the old man talked a lot. He went on and on as if he had crammed everything into a bag and was now hesitantly taking things out to show us. Maybe it was the pelting rain and wind that did it.

When he returned from the war, he did not go home. He covered his trail, without contacting his wife to explain why he was leaving. He did not even tell her that he was alive and had been discharged from the army. His wife's name was Yayoi. She probably uses her maiden name now. Yayoi Koko. "A pretty name, isn't it?" the old man had said.

"She was gentle and good-natured, though, so someone probably married her." Then the old man had lain down and promptly gone to sleep. Or perhaps he was just pretending to sleep. We couldn't tell.

"I've been thinking." Kawabe stops in the middle of the road and rummages around in his cram-school bag. "Here. Take a look at this," he says, handing me a folded piece of white paper. I open it up. It's the vocabulary test that the teacher gave back today. Twenty-five out of a hundred. "Oooh," I say sympathetically. "That's pretty bad, all right." Kawabe looks puzzled, then takes a quick glance at the paper and snatches it back.

"Not that one! This one. This one here."

The second piece of paper has five names and telephone numbers written in Kawabe's very eccentric handwriting. And the surname of every one is . . . Koko.

"I looked them up. Yesterday."

Since the day of the typhoon we have begun to meet at the old man's house again. But I remember now that

Kawabe didn't come yesterday. When cram school finished, he said he had something to do and hurried home without even stopping at the bakery.

"I had to go to the phone company to find the numbers in downtown Tokyo. After all, the old man did say that she came from the downtown area."

"So what are these for?"

"We're going to call them." Kawabe's voice rises a tone.

"But there's no Yayoi here," Yamashita says.

Kawabe draws himself up and speaks pompously, as though giving a lecture. "My dear boy, the telephone book lists only the head of household. Perhaps Yayoi is a resident of one of these households, perhaps not. But we may be able to get a clue as to her whereabouts by calling. Koko is, after all, a very unusual surname."

It takes me about five seconds to realize what Kawabe means by the head of household. His shrill voice made it sound like some kind of technical word.

"I see . . . Well done, Kawabe!" Yamashita's little eyes blink rapidly and he looks at Kawabe in admiration.

"I couldn't figure out which phone book to use at first. It was pretty confusing," Kawabe says proudly. Hmph! Little show-off.

"Well, it won't be much use if she lives outside Tokyo," I say. For some reason I feel like I have to cut him down to size.

"So? We'll just look it up again. The phone company has books listing all the numbers for the whole country." The little brat is just bursting with confidence.

"What if she remarried? Her name will have changed."

"Oh well . . ."

"And some people aren't even in the phone book."

Kawabe falls silent. Then suddenly he bursts out, "That's why I said we could at least get some kind of clue, right? After all, we might find some relative of hers!" he yells in frustration. "Anyway, we're going to call. Meet at my house!"

We sit hunched around the telephone at Kawabe's house, glaring at each other. "Okay. Let's do it," Kawabe says. Yamashita and I nod. We nod, but nobody makes a move to pick up the receiver. Silence.

"Okay. Let's do it," Kawabe says again. Yamashita and I nod. Silence.

The phone rings suddenly. All three of us jump. Kawabe picks up the phone. It's his mother.

"Yeah. You're going to be home late tonight . . . Yes . . . Uh-huh, I know . . . Yeah, I'll be all right. Yes, I'll eat properly . . . Okay. 'Bye."

Kawabe hangs up the phone and breathes a sigh of relief, then turns to me and says, "You do it."

"What are you talking about? It's your phone!"

"So what. You're the best at this kind of thing." Kawabe is an expert escape artist. I poke Yamashita.

"Me? Call someone I don't even know? I'd blow it for sure."

I am certain to blow it, too, but there doesn't seem to be anything I can do about it. I pick up the receiver. For some reason I always seem to be the one who ends up doing this kind of thing.

No one answers at the first phone number.

"No answer," I say, and hang up.

"What are you looking so relieved for? Next one."

"You do the next one, Kawabe."

"No, you do it."

I pick up the phone again. It has hardly started ringing when a man answers.

"Hello?" He sounds annoyed.

"Umm. Hello?"

"Hello?"

"Is this Mr. Koko?"

"Yes." He sounds even more annoyed.

"We're looking for a Miss Yayoi Koko . . ."

"What?" He is really mad. I want to hang up.

"Is there a Miss Yayoi Koko living there?"

"Yayoi?"

"She's an elderly lady. We're looking for her."

"Well, she doesn't live here." The phone goes dead.

"He says she doesn't live there."

Yamashita crosses the name off the list. "This is the next one," he says.

"Me again?"

"Sure, why not? Just do it like the last time." Yamashita slaps me on the shoulders.

This time a woman answers. I think she must be about my mother's age.

"Yayoi Koko? That must be my relative."

"Really?" Holding the receiver in one hand I strike a victory pose with the other, raising my fist into the air triumphantly. Kawabe and Yamashita bring their heads closer.

"I'm looking for her."

"Really? Why?"

"Uhm, well . . . My grandfather wants to meet her."

"Your grandfather?"

". . . Ye-yes."

"Why?"

"Huh?"

"Why does your grandfather want to meet Yayoi Koko?"

"Uhmm . . ."

The woman suddenly lowers her voice. "It's a secret, is it?" I can't blow it now.

"Well, my grandfather wants to apologize to her. He's dying. He might even die tomorrow." I am a liar, after all.

"Oh? That's terrible." She exhales slowly. She must be smoking. "You said apologize? You mean he ran off and left her?"

"N-no, nothing like that." She laughs as though something is funny.

I am flustered. "Uh, could you put her on the phone?"

"Who?"

"Yayoi Koko."

"But she doesn't live here." The woman sounds very surprised. "I live alone."

"Well, where is she, then?"

"I don't know."

"But you said she was your relative."

"All I meant was that we must be related somehow, because Koko is a very unusual name. I'm sorry, but I don't know any old lady called Yayoi Koko."

I sigh in disappointment.

"You can call me anytime, though," the woman says, and hangs up.

On the third phone number I get an answering machine. A man's voice whispers to the sounds of cowboy music, "I will be gone for a while. I don't know when I'm coming back, but I will be praying for your happiness as I journey on." Gross.

On the fourth try, a little girl answers the phone.

"Hello. Nobody's home," she says in a loud voice. She has trouble getting her tongue around some of the words.

"Your mommy's not home?"

"She's at work."

Maybe I should call back later, I think.

"Gen can't play today 'cuz he's got a cough. I'm here with Grandma."

"Your grandma is there?" I ask in surprise.

"Grandma's deaf. She can't answer the phone. Who is speaking, please?" she adds as though suddenly remembering her phone manners.

"I'm a friend of your grandma's." I really am a liar.

"Grandma's friend?" the girl repeats as though it seems very strange. "Grandma has friends?"

"Do you know your grandma's name? It's Yayoi, isn't it? Ya-yo-i." I say each syllable very carefully, trying to contain my excitement.

"No, it's not," the girl retorts simply. "Her name's Hanae. Ha-na-e."

I am crushed and signal failure to Kawabe and Yamashita.

"Are you really Grandma's friend?"

I am about to apologize for my mistake and hang up when the little girl says, "Are you Grandma Yayoi's friend?"

"Huh?"

"Grandma Yayoi isn't here."

"But your grandma's name is Hanae, isn't it?" I am totally confused.

"Grandma Yayoi is much older than Grandma Hanae. Grandma Hanae is Daddy's mommy. Grandma Yayoi is Grandpa's sister. She's really old, so she doesn't live here."

I am even more confused. "Then where is she? I mean Grandma Yayoi."

"She was here. But now it's my brother's room. He has to study. So I have to be quiet."

"You mean Grandma Yayoi used to live with you?"

"My name's Mayu."

"Well, Mayu, Grandma Yayoi used to live with you, right?"

She doesn't answer. I wonder if I have said something wrong.

"Used-to-live-with-you?" she asks uncertainly.

"Grandma Yayoi stayed in your house with you?" For the first time in my life I am using a coaxing voice.

"Uh-huh."

"And where is she now?"

"To-ju-Nur-sing-Home," she answers vigorously. "My mommy says it's a very nice place."

The nursing home is like a small hospital. Old men and women play chess, watch TV, and practice hula dancing in white, air-conditioned, boxlike rooms. Everyone is very quiet. Surrounded by the racket of Hawaiian guitar music and TV commercials, the old people make no sound, talking only in whispers and walking quietly. It is as if they are moving in water. In the midst of this, someone who looks like a nurse wearing a pale-pink uniform walks toward us, the rubber soles of her shoes squeaking on the floor.

"And what can I do for you?" she asks. She looks like a college student. Her hair is neatly bobbed just below her ears.

"Is Miss Yayoi Koko here?" I ask.

"She doesn't have an appointment with anyone today," she says, glancing at a bulletin board on the wall. "Did you come to visit her?"

When I nod she says, "It's such a long way. That's really kind of you." It was a long way. We had to ride on the train for two hours and then take a bus in order to get here.

"You came all the way to visit her?" she says in admiration. "Are you her grandson?"

Kawabe and Yamashita poke me.

"I'm the grandson of her sister-in-law, Hanae." I can't seem to stop lying.

"This way," she says and, turning on her heel, strides down the corridor, her shoes squeaking again.

"Uhm . . ."

"Yes?" The woman looks back at me.

"We can go by ourselves, if you'd just tell us where she is." Once we meet Yayoi Koko, the truth will come out. But the young woman just says, "It's all right. Follow me," and keeps on walking. We seem to have no choice.

It is a long corridor. From the window we can see farm fields and in the middle a big power station. Countless electric cables hang motionless in the hot summer glare as though holding their breath.

"Miss Koko, you have visitors." The young woman

opens the door at the very end of the corridor. We huddle in the doorway, trying to make ourselves small.

"It's your sister's grandson. You used to live together, remember? He's brought some friends with him. Isn't that nice?" the young woman says, and gives me a pat on the shoulder. Then she pulls me inside, saying, "Come on in."

A small, thin woman sits on the bed. She is smiling.

"You haven't seen him for a long time, so he must have grown a lot since then. Do you remember?"

"Yes, yes." The old woman smiles.

"Well, then, take your time," the young woman says. She fluffs up the pillows with a few deft blows, sits us down on the sofa, and leaves the room. She seems very busy. Left behind in the room, we feel like we're cushions on the sofa.

The old woman slowly stretches out one arm, takes three sweets wrapped in paper out of a drawer beside the bed, and offers them to us. I take them and sit back down, giving one to Kawabe and one to Yamashita.

"There's tea in the lobby," she says.

"I'm not thirsty," I say. In fact, my throat is parched.

The old woman keeps right on smiling. I wonder if she really believes I am Mayu's older brother. Her skin is very fair. She has lots of wrinkles, but her little round eyes seem very kind.

The paper wrapping the sweet is starting to get damp in my hand. I don't know what to talk about.

"I'll go get some tea," Kawabe says, rising from the sofa.

"Me, too," Yamashita says, hurrying after him. It is always this way. I am always just a little too slow.

"Uh."

"Yes?" The old woman nods gently and stares straight at me. The pattern of tiny flowers on her gown seems to waver for a moment in a slight breeze.

"Grandma Yayoi," I begin again.

"Yes?"

"Er, are you well?"

"Yes, thank you." She nods, bowing her head with her white hair tied in a bun at the back. Conversation ceases.

"Mayu is very well," I say, even though I have never met the girl. I am trying desperately to get a conversation going.

"Yes."

"Mayu is very well," I repeat.

"Really? That's nice. It's very hot this year. It's hard on us old folks." She does not seem to have any further interest in Mayu.

I steel myself. "I'd like to talk to you about something that happened a long time ago."

"Yes, yes. Go ahead." She nods happily.

"Once, long ago, there was a man who went to war. He had a wife, but even when the war was over he did not go home. He had not forgotten her. He still lives all alone, even now," I say, all in one breath.

"Many things happened, even after the war ended," the old woman says, closing her eyes gently. "I'm sure things like that must have happened, too."

She rubs the back of one hand. Those dark, gnarled hands do not match this tiny, fair-skinned woman. She keeps her head down, staring at her hands.

112

"This man, during the war, he had a terrible experience. It was so bad he could not go home . . ." I am at a loss for words. What should I do? "Do you think that he was bad?"

"Do I think so?" she asks slowly. She looks cautious. I should never have come, I think. All we had thought about was finding her. We should have realized that she might not like it.

But her anxiety seems to melt away, and she tilts her head and looks at me.

"You want to know whether I would blame him if I were his wife?"

"Yes."

She thinks for a while. It seems like she is enjoying the question.

"I'm sure I would not blame him. There would be no point. Besides, I always forget anything bad that happens to me." She is smiling again. "War is not normal. It could easily change someone like that."

"Could I bring him here? If he said he wanted to come?"

"Who?"

I tell her the old man's name. She falls silent, thinking. Maybe she does not want to meet him.

"You know," she finally says, "my memory is not so good these days. Who did you say he was?" She smiles uncertainly.

When I tell her that he is her husband, she laughs as if she thinks this very funny and says, "My husband died a long time ago."

"She must have gone senile," I say when we have left the nursing home. The sun is sinking lower in the sky. A cool breeze brushes past us. The first sign of autumn, I think.

"Maybe she's the wrong person," Yamashita says. I shake my head.

"She's Mayu's great-aunt, right? But when I talked about Mayu, she didn't seem to really understand."

"But," Kawabe says and lowers his voice, "it's also possible that she just pretended to forget because she doesn't want to meet the old man."

"Hmmm." I think for a minute. "In either case, it's probably better if the old man doesn't meet her, right?"

"Yeah, I guess so," Kawabe agrees reluctantly.

"Hey!" Yamashita stops suddenly. "Look!"

We look back. The beige building is dyed a fiery orange by the rays of the setting sun. Someone is waving from one of the windows. The glass windowpane looks like the surface of a pond rippled by an evening breeze.

"Maybe it's the nurse."

"No, it isn't." It was the old woman.

We wave back with all our might. She waves slowly and carefully, in measured strokes, with one elbow bent. I can't see her face, but I am sure that she is smiling.

It is a sight too lonely for words. In the middle of the fields dyed with the evening light, the little boxlike building stands all alone. That box is jammed full of something that I want to understand better, but it seems to drift farther and farther away. Just like time, which we can never stop.

The old woman stops waving and stands at the window watching us.

"I'll be back!" I shout. But I know that she cannot hear me. She turns away from the window and disappears.

"Let's come back again," I say.

"Yeah, let's," Yamashita and Kawabe agree, as the light of the setting sun soaks deep inside them.

10

Despite the raging typhoon, our cosmos survived. Their stems, which were limp and bent, once again stretch upward. They have more leaves and seem to be an even darker green.

"They don't give up, do they?" Kawabe says in admiration.

We gather every day after cram school at the old man's house as if it is a meeting place. We check on how the cosmos are doing and then do our homework. It isn't like the old man goes out of his way to welcome us or anything, but he doesn't look unhappy to see us, either. And before we know it, there are four cushions out on the floor, their cotton stuffing flattened with use, wearing stiffly ironed white cotton covers.

"What do you plan to do with all that studying when you're so stupid?"

"It's because we're so stupid that we have to study!"

The old man and Kawabe often have such exchanges. But when it comes to history or writing, he teaches us a lot. Thanks to the old man, even Yamashita is getting better at writing.

One day he told us his version of an event in Japanese history. The great warrior Yoshitsune Minamoto was supposed to have committed suicide after losing a final battle. But according to the old man, he had actually escaped to Hokkaido, crossed over to Asia, and wreaked havoc as the Mongolian conqueror Genghis Khan. On our way home that evening, I tell the others something that has been nagging me.

"You remember the old lady at the nursing home?"

"Yayoi Koko?"

"Doesn't she remind you of someone?"

Kawabe and Yamashita look at each other with puzzled expressions.

"Who?"

"You don't know?"

"Ah!" Yamashita looks at me.

"You see!"

"Yeah, they do look alike."

"Who?!" Kawabe still doesn't get it.

"The lady at the seed shop."

"That old lady?"

"Don't you think they look alike?"

"Yeah, they do."

We have not told the old man that we met Yayoi Koko at the nursing home.

"What do you think? Should we ask the lady at the seed shop to do us a favor?"

"What favor?"

I tell them my idea.

When we take the seed lady to his house and introduce her as Miss Koko, the old man looks like he's seen a ghost. We got her to come by saying that we wanted to show her how the cosmos were growing; then along the way to his house we explained that we wanted her to pretend she was Yayoi Koko. Of course, we told her why, explaining that the old man must want to meet her and talk with her after all these years.

"I think he will be very happy," I said.

"I wonder," the old woman said, and thought for a while. "Do you really think he will believe that I am Yayoi Koko?"

"No problem. You look just like her. You're small and fair, and your forehead is round."

The old lady put her hand to her forehead and smoothed out some of the wrinkles. "Have you boys thought this through very carefully?"

"Yes."

"All right, then. As long as you have really thought about it. All I have to tell him is that I don't think badly of him, is that correct?"

"That's correct," Yamashita replied.

So now the old man is standing stock-still in the middle of the garden, still holding the laundry tub. The old lady bows stiffly, as though uncomfortable. The old man's long underwear, which has just been hung up to dry, is flapping in the breeze.

"Why don't you have a seat over here," Yamashita

says from the porch. He sets out two glasses of chilled barley tea.

The old man doesn't even look at Yamashita. He walks toward the porch scowling and suddenly turns and invites the woman to have a seat. Then, still holding the laundry tub firmly, he sits down with a thump right on top of the lighted mosquito coil.

"Ow!"

The old lady giggles and the old man scowls even more. I wave at Yamashita that we should leave. This is no time for outsiders.

The next day after cram school we go to the old man's house as usual, bringing some bread with us for lunch. The old man is ironing. He doesn't say a word. The room is filled with the heat of summer and the smells of clean clothes and steam.

The old man sprays mist on the white cushion cover and presses it. He smooths out each wrinkle, pressing firmly, puts the iron on its stand, moves the cover a little, and mists it again. Blue veins stand out on the hand that grips the iron. We suggest that it is too hot to iron right now. Why not do it later and have lunch first? If he doesn't have anything in the house, we can go shopping for him, or perhaps he would like us to cook up a fried egg. But he ignores us.

Kawabe can't stand it any longer. "So, how did it go? Yesterday, I mean."

The old man unplugs the iron and begins to put the stiffly starched cover on a torn cushion which has stuffing coming out. He does not say a word. We look at each other.

"Didn't you want to meet her?" Yamashita asks

timidly. When the old man still doesn't answer, Yamashita looks at me accusingly, all but saying that it is my fault for thinking up such a crazy idea.

"Are you mad at us?" I am a bit peeved. The old man piles up the four cushions, looking like new in their freshly ironed covers, and gives me the once-over.

"Before she left, she begged me not to scold you."

"You guessed right away?"

"Of course."

"And so you're angry?"

He puts his elbow on the pile of cushions and reclines. "You made her tell a lie. That's called fraud, you know."

"It's not fraud!" Kawabe protests. He always has exploded easily.

"Damn fools!"

The seat of my pants rises at least three inches off the floor. It is the first time I have ever heard him speak like that.

"We didn't mean any harm," I say.

"That's not the point."

"Well, what is the point?" Kawabe is still protesting.

"You don't play tricks with a person's life."

I feel awful hearing him say that about us in such a disillusioned voice. It is much worse than being told I am ugly or stupid or boring.

"I thought it was such a good idea," I say. "They look so much alike."

There is a long silence. I look up suddenly, wondering what is wrong. The old man is glaring at me.

"What do you mean?"

120   I finally realize that I have blown it.

"What do you mean 'they look alike'?"

Kawabe is glaring at me, too. "Kiyama, you idiot."

Yamashita shakes his head as if to say we are finished.

"We went to meet Yayoi Koko," I reply. I have no choice.

"You found her?"

"Yes."

I tell him the story from the beginning. How we phoned people. About the nursing home. About how she had lived with her brother and his son's family before entering the home.

"And was she well?" I can see only the top of his balding head.

"Yes."

"Did she say anything?"

When I don't answer, the old man raises his face and looks steadily at me.

"She's forgotten."

"I see."

"She's gone senile. She thinks her husband died a long time ago."

The old man laughs a little. "I guess she's right. It's as good as being dead, anyway."

"But it was different."

The humming of the cicadas becomes a whirlpool of sound, enveloping us. My ears are full of the overlapping voices of millions of insects, making my own voice sound like it's coming from far away, like it's somebody else that's talking.

"She thinks her dead husband is a hero. A hero. She told me that her husband carried a bomb on his back into the midst of the enemy. She told me in great detail, as if she had seen it with her own eyes. It was so real, it was hard to believe it was a lie."

"You can't call that lying," Kawabe says.

"No, you're right. It isn't lying," the old man says, still looking down. "Was it far away, that place?"

"A little."

But then the old man turns his back on me and growls, "I wish you'd mind your own business!"

"Is anyone home?" a frail, trembling voice asks. Looking out from the porch, I see the lady from the seed shop standing by the front door. "Oh! You boys are here, too," she says as she comes into the garden walking toward the porch. She is wearing a kimono today, and carries a white parasol. The sunlight pools on top of it so that it looks like a piece has been cut out of the sky. Like the entrance to another world.

She folds the parasol and bows politely, saying, "Excuse me for bothering you yesterday." Then she looks at us and says, "I'm sorry I didn't do a very good job."

The three of us apologize hoarsely.

"Oh no. Now, really. It is I who must apologize," she protests, and bows again.

The old man comes onto the porch. "I am very sorry for the trouble we caused you," he mumbles, and offers her one of the cushions with a newly ironed cover.

She sits down, placing a package wrapped in a pale-pink cloth on the porch. She opens the cloth and we see a colander filled with red berries.

"Raspberries! Wow!"

"My relatives in the country sent them. It's only a few," she says, smiling.

Having been ordered to wash them, I stand in the kitchen and put some water in a bowl. I add a little salt and wash the berries gently, one by one. It was the old man who taught me to use salt when washing fruit. The berries are like clusters of tiny rubies, each a slightly different shade of red. I rinse them carefully and carry them out to the porch.

"Mmmm, sweet!"

"Mmmm, sour!"

"Mmmm, good!" we exclaim simultaneously.

"Bears would love these," the old man says, rolling a berry around in his mouth. He seems back to normal.

"Bears?"

"Bears love berries. Wherever you find a good patch of berries, you'll find bears. And a good place for finding bears is a good place for berries."

The red fruit bursts sweet and tangy in my mouth. If you gathered the dew from the leaves in a forest untouched by man, it would taste like this, I think.

"Wild grapes, too," the old woman says.

"That's right, wild grapes," the old man says contentedly, as if he wouldn't mind becoming a bear himself.

"And mulberries."

"That's right." The old man is getting dreamy-eyed, like a cat who has eaten too much catnip.

"Or yew berries."

The old man sighs blissfully and falls silent.

"But they're getting smaller, and there are fewer and fewer places where you can find them." The old woman eats each berry as though sucking nectar, her tiny mouth pursed like a little bird's.

123

"Where are you from?" the old man asks.

"Hokkaido. Aibetsu."

"Really? I'm from Toma."

"Well, well," the old lady says in surprise. "We're neighbors." She is smiling. When she smiles, she looks just like Yayoi Koko. "I had a feeling that we might be neighbors when I met you yesterday."

"Oh."

"People from Hokkaido are a little different, aren't they?"

The old man nods emphatically. "Hokkaido girls are hard workers, too, like my mother," he says.

"That's right!" Kawabe looks up. "You had a mother once, too." He seems strangely impressed.

"Of course I did!"

"Yes, Hokkaido girls do work hard. They're very energetic," the old lady agrees, and then laughs, a little embarrassed.

The two of them talk for a long time. They talk about skiing to school with rubber boots for ski boots, about the old man's work as a railway engineer, about a secret place for gathering wild grapes, about pickling a whole potful of dried herring roe, about swimming in the river in summer and how cold the water was, about a prisoner who escaped from Ashibari prison and was caught right before the little old lady's eyes, about how the whole family spent a day hanging up sardines to dry, about eating rice with green chili peppers pickled in soy sauce and how delicious it was, about how the old lady hated soft fresh herring roe, about how lonely the cry of a fox sounded when it wandered down from the mountain at night, about how all kinds of flowers burst into bloom in summer, about the incredible amount of steam rising from the horses that pulled the lumber carts from the forest in winter, about the day set aside for cleaning charcoal heaters, about how they sprinkled sugar on frozen milk and ate it, about making a ski jump by piling up snow and competing to see how far they could jump . . . They talk and talk, and still the stories keep coming.

I am amazed at how much is stored up inside these two people. Maybe it is fun to grow old. The older you get, the more memories you have. And even if the owner of the memories passes away, maybe the memories themselves continue on, floating through the air, melting in the rain, and soaking into the earth. Maybe after wandering through many places they slip inside somebody else's heart. Maybe it's the mischief-making of someone else's memory that makes us feel as if we have been somewhere before even though we know it is the first time.

The two fall silent and sit gazing at the garden. They look like they have lived together for ages as husband and wife. A cool breeze wafts past. It feels as if we are all enveloped within a tiny globule of a tangy-sweet ripe raspberry soaked in sunlight and forest wind.

11

My mother pokes at a piece of lettuce and goes back to drinking her wine. A hamburger grilled to perfection, glazed carrots looking too good to be real. But for some reason they don't have any flavor.

"Why don't you eat?" I say, putting down my chopsticks. As usual, my mother is just watching me absently.

"I don't really want hamburger." She nibbles a bit of cracker as though bored. It makes a dry, crunching noise and she washes it down with a gulp of wine. That's all she eats every day, but still she has put on weight. Her eyelids seem swollen and she walks around slowly, as though carrying something very heavy.

I leave the table and open the refrigerator in the

kitchen. There is some wilted lettuce, a moldy squash, and three golden juicy-looking pears in the vegetable compartment.

"You bought some pears?"

"Mmm," she answers from the other side of the counter. "I thought they looked good, but . . ."

"Why don't you eat them, then?"

"I don't feel like it anymore."

When I take a knife out from under the sink, my mother comes into the kitchen and tries to take it and the pears away from me.

"It's all right, Mom," I say, and begin peeling swiftly. As the white, juicy flesh appears, a ribbon of gold peel unwinds from the pear.

"You're good!" My mother watches my hands in surprise.

I have peeled lots of pears at the old man's place. "Keep your right thumb firmly on the knife," he told me. And when I did, I was able to get the knife to move slowly forward. The first time I managed to peel a pear all by myself, taking a long time to do it, what was left of the pear was all crooked. The old man ate that pear (which, as Yamashita pointed out, came complete with my fingerprints) as though it were the best thing he'd ever tasted.

Now the smooth, round pear turns slowly in my hands, covering them with juice. When it is completely peeled, I give it to my mother.

"It's delicious!" she exclaims. A drop of juice slips down her wrist and hangs precariously from her elbow. Another drop follows it and then another. Standing in the kitchen at night watching my mother absorbed in eating that pear, for some reason I feel like crying. I grip the knife and begin slowly peeling another one.

Before I know it, she has eaten them all. And she doesn't drink any more that night.

We take a train with the old man. It is the first time that we have gone anywhere with him.

"I wonder where we're going."

"I don't know."

The old man is carrying a big paper shopping bag in one hand and holding on to a strap with the other. On the way to the train station, he strode along briskly, his back straight, and he just laughed, "He-henh," when we followed after him, pestering him like noisy chickens, asking, "Where are we going? What are you doing?"

He had been busy all afternoon tying many round black balls together with some kind of string. When we tried to touch them, he just said, "Don't touch." Then he said, "Come back tonight." So Kawabe and I told our mothers we were going to study at Yamashita's house and Yamashita told his mother that he would be studying at my house.

We get off the train at the third stop, just after crossing over a bridge.

"Maybe we're going to the river," Kawabe says. "I came here once to catch tadpoles. And there was a tadpole as big as the palm of my hand. My dad told me it would turn into a bullfrog."

Kawabe glances behind him. The dark riverbank spreads out on the other side of the platform. Then we begin going down the stairs. Kawabe gazes absently at a big advertisement for a department store. "This station is a lot cleaner now," he remarks.

"Hey, where are we going?" Yamashita asks the old man impatiently. "You won't tell us anything."

As Kawabe guessed, we are going to the river. The old man makes us wait at the top of the embankment while he takes the shopping bag and climbs down to the grassy strip beside the river. He doesn't come back for a long time.

Yamashita and Kawabe go off to explore. Bored, I lie down on the riverbank. One star sheds a faint light as it gazes down on me. There are only ten days of summer holiday left. What am I doing here?

"Eek!" A woman's shriek is followed by a man's voice roaring, "What do you think you're doing?!" I sit up abruptly, looking in the direction the voices come from. A car is parked in the dark on the road beside the bank. A man is standing in front of the car holding on to somebody's collar. It is Yamashita. Kawabe is standing rigidly beside him.

"What?! Another one?" the man says, staring at me as I come panting up. He is wearing a black-and-white zebra-striped sport shirt and his hair is cut very short. His shadowy face makes him look diabolic.

"Little brats. Peeking in my car!"

"We didn't! It's all a mistake!" Kawabe stands as stiff as a wax figure and then suddenly begins jiggling.

"Shut up! Just what were you doing, then?"

Kawabe's jiggling stops abruptly and he freezes again.

Looking around, I see cars parked a careful twenty feet apart all down the road. But nobody gets out. The **129** cars must all be full of couples making out. Disgusting.

"Uh, we—" I begin hesitantly.

"What?" Sport Shirt glares at me while twisting Yamashita's collar tighter.

"Argh!" Yamashita gurgles.

A girl gets out of the car. Her clothes are all rumpled. "Why don't you just forget it?" she says, combing her hair back with her fingers.

"Shut up!"

The girl rolls her eyes and leans against the car. She doesn't say anything.

"We came with our grandfather." There doesn't seem to be any other choice, so I keep talking.

"And where is he, then? Let's settle this once and for all."

It looks like we're in trouble. Plus I have to go to the bathroom. What is the old man doing? He's the one who went off and left us here.

"Oh!" The girl looks up at the sky, her mouth open.

"Eh?" Sport Shirt looks up, too. Then a lively sound echoes along the riverbank. *Pop! Pop!* Fireworks!

They follow one after another. Maybe not as elaborate a display as the fireworks festival our town puts on, but splendid just the same, like red, green, and yellow chrysanthemums blooming in the sky. And it is very different from watching them at a festival crowded with people.

"That's lovely," the girl says in admiration. People begin to get out of the other cars.

"It's the old man!" Kawabe says. "I never knew he could make fireworks."

130   "Impossible."

"But it must be. Those black balls. They were filled with gunpowder. I've seen them on TV."

"You mean your grandfather is doing that?" Sport Shirt asks us, his eyes wide with surprise.

"Yup," Kawabe says with a swagger.

"He's pretty good," the man remarks, and then he hastily releases Yamashita's collar, saying, "Whoops! Sorry. I forgot."

The fireworks go up in six volleys. A flower in full bloom bursts into the night sky, and as it slowly falls like drops of water, another flower blooms. And as the second flower melts into darkness, a new flower opens. I watch every step of the display. I don't want to miss any of it, not even the last second.

"He wanted us to see this," Yamashita says, his eyes still fixed on the sky. "Of course, he would want to show us. After all, it's fantastic!"

"My dad was a fireworks expert," Kawabe says.

"This is summer. Really summer," Sport Shirt says, and the girl says, "Mmmm," nodding in agreement.

The fireworks finally fade, and we stand for a long moment in the sudden silence staring up at the night sky. Then Kawabe starts running down the bank. "Race you!"

We dash toward the old man as he walks slowly in our direction along the dark stretch of grass beside the river.

Sport Shirt insists that he wants to treat the old man to a beer and takes us all out to an okonomiyaki restaurant. It is full of grownups drinking beer. Yamashita and I are a little nervous and say, "Let's go home." But Kawabe says, "I've been here with my mother," and sits down without hesitation. The tables with their built-in hot plates for cooking are so unusual that we find ourselves sitting down, too.

"Order whatever you like," Sport Shirt says. He is in a great mood.

"All right, then, I'll have one ginger and one squid batter. And some orange juice, too." Kawabe has no compunctions.

The old man, Sport Shirt, and the girl drink beer. It's the first time I have seen the old man talk with other adults away from home. I expect him to be a bit gruff and unfriendly, so it is a surprise to see him enjoying himself. He chatters about how he had worked in a fireworks factory when he was young, and how after the war he had worked at many different jobs in such places as a car repair shop and a tree nursery.

We cook the okonomiyaki following Kawabe's instructions. Each serving comes in its own small bowl. First we mix the egg into the batter, which is full of chopped cabbage and other things. Then we spread the batter on the hot griddle that's built into the middle of the table. We sprinkle fish flakes on top and then flip it over to cook the other side. When it's done, we coat it with sauce and powdered seaweed and serve it to the three adults. We make our own, listening to their talk while we eat, and then cook some more. It keeps us pretty busy.

"You must have had a hard time, what with the war and all," Sport Shirt says.

"And what do you do?" the old man asks.

"I run a pachinko parlor. I don't own it, I just get paid to run it," he says, laughing a little sheepishly, embarrassed to be talking about gambling in front of us kids. "Lately we've had some strange customers. They dress like bank clerks but talk like gangsters. They drive me nuts."

"Hmm. Sounds like hard work," Kawabe remarks, stuffing his mouth with food.

"Yeah. It's the one right across from the station. Why don't you come around and play for a while?"

"When I grow up, I will," Kawabe says, gulping down his juice and giving a long sigh of satisfaction.

"And what about you guys?" The conversation suddenly swings around to focus on us. "What are you going to do when you grow up?"

"I'm going to run a fish store," Yamashita says, chewing on a mouthful of pork. "Like my father."

"Very impressive," Sport Shirt says loudly.

"I'm going to make fireworks. I decided that just now," Kawabe says, and the old man gives a great belly laugh. "Ah-ha-ha!" He laughs so loud that Sport Shirt almost drops his tankard of beer.

"And you?"

What do I want to be? "I don't know yet," I answer.

"Well, it doesn't matter what you do. Just do it well," Sport Shirt says, and then adds with a rueful laugh, "Not that I should talk." The girl laughs, too.

"You kids are all right. I'm sorry I didn't realize that earlier," he continues, his eyes a little bleary from drinking. "But"—he pokes the girl beside him—"when I thought you might be taking a peek at her, I lost my head."

"Hey, it's okay," Yamashita says, blushing bright red.

Sport Shirt nods solemnly and says, "But she's pretty good-looking, isn't she? Stacked. Here. Give them another look." And he gives her blouse a tug.

"Cut that out!" She looks mad, but her voice is laughing. The three of us stare at the floor.

"If she's so important to you, why don't you marry her?" the old man says.

"Her?" Sport Shirt exclaims, his voice shrill with surprise. He points at the girl as though stunned. The girl gives him a sidelong look, rather annoyed.

"That might not be a bad idea," Sport Shirt says, and then yells, "Beer!" The girl's big eyes blink a little and she looks down. She is very pretty.

"When we get married, old man, you'll have to make us a big fireworks display," Sport Shirt says, taking a long pull from his tankard.

"Right!" the old man says, sipping his beer. "It's a deal." He is in great spirits tonight.

"Cheers!" yells Kawabe, raising his glass of juice high in the air.

12

Soccer camp begins the last week in August. Every year we go to the coach's home island and spend four days practicing soccer and swimming in the ocean.

There are twenty-seven of us, including the fourth-, fifth-, and sixth-graders and the coach. Everyone has to get up early to meet at the train station. When I get there, the place is already in an uproar, with fifth-graders wearing knapsacks running around on the platform and fourth-graders crying because they don't want to leave their mothers. And Kawabe adds to the racket by shouting with eager bossiness, "Fall in!"

We travel to the island by bullet train and ferry, and then get on a bus and head for the inn. The white ribbon of road winds between a sheer cliff and the foaming whitecaps of the ocean. The water near the horizon swells and moves toward us, turning into waves as it nears the shore. Wave after wave after wave. It is like the slow breathing of some enormous creature. I wonder how many times the earth has breathed since it was born, and for how long waves will continue to roll across the sea.

The horizon curves in a wide arc as though beckoning us to come nearer, yet always moving on ahead of us. No matter how far we go, there is no way we will ever reach it. I sit back in my seat. The bus is quiet now. After getting up so early, everyone has fallen asleep. The few local passengers have already gotten off and we are the only ones left in the care of the bus, which rocks us like a cradle. I feel like staying on the bus forever, chasing the horizon.

"What're you thinking about?" the coach asks. He is sitting beside me. When he isn't coaching, he teaches painting. He has wide shoulders, thighs as round as logs, and a thick beard. He looks just like a big bear. He leans over to look out the window and I catch the scent of oranges.

"Graveyards."

"Huh?" The coach looks at me.

"There are a lot of graveyards, don't you think? So near the sea. Won't they be washed away?"

Tombstones crowd the tops of some of the rocks sticking out of the ocean. Some stones are old and chipped, while others are brand-new. Why didn't I notice them last year when I came?

"It's a good place," the coach says. "You can look out over the sea. When I die, I'd like to be buried someplace like that."

"There're a lot of them, aren't there?"

"Uh-huh." The coach nods, and looks out the window for a while. "There are hardly any people living on the island. The young people like me have all left. Only the tombstones are increasing."

"Hmmm." The words "Grave Island" float in my mind. But this place is not at all gloomy. The bus rounds a big curve and the sea rushes up as if biting into the shore. Aha! More graves.

"It's almost as if they're protecting the island," I say. "The people in the graves, I mean."

"Yeah, I see what you mean."

The dead sleep between the sea and the land where people dwell. Silently, forever, breathing deeply of the sea wind.

"You're in sixth grade, so this year will be your last."

"Yes."

The coach closes his eyes. The sound of the waves ebbs and flows, mingling with the noise of the engine as the bus climbs a hill.

The bus keeps on going. A single moth flutters around a garish fluorescent light, brushing powder from its wings. It is pitch-black outside the window, impossible to see where the bus is going. The road must be getting worse, because the bus shakes violently, but it runs on silently as though all sound has been crushed by the darkness. I am sitting by myself in the middle seat at the very back of the bus. Everyone else must be sleeping.

"Ah!"

I see someone's reflection in the window. Me? It should be me, but it isn't. It is someone very old, a 137 stranger. An old person I have never seen before. Yet somehow the face looks familiar . . .

The bus begins to bounce even more and I can't get near the window. I can't see the face clearly. Who can it be? Is it stuck on the bus outside the window? Or else . . . I look for my own reflection in the window, but the bouncing of the bus becomes even worse. I fall off the seat and my knee breaks with a snap.

"Kiyama . . . Kiyama . . ."

I start awake, and in the dim glow of the night-light I see an old, stained wooden ceiling. Kawabe is shaking my shoulder. Now I remember. We are at soccer camp. This is the inn run by the coach's mother and father.

"Wake up, Kiyama!" Kawabe whispers hoarsely. There are three fourth-graders sleeping in the room with Kawabe, Yamashita, and me.

"What do you want?"

"He has to pee."

"Who?"

"Yamashita."

"Well, why doesn't he go, then?"

"He's afraid to go alone."

"So go with him."

"I am. But don't you need to go, too?"

"No."

"Come on."

Oh great, I think, getting up reluctantly. It's not like I'm not a little afraid, too. I mean, this is a creepy old place. I guess it seems like we should have outgrown our fear of the dark by now. But maybe that's something that never really leaves you.

Yamashita is already at the door fidgeting. "Hurry. I'm going to burst!" he whispers.

One of the thick double doors to the hall outside our room has been left ajar. This used to be a miso warehouse, we were told. It was turned into an inn after the coach's great-grandfather died. The small rooms with their tiny windows and thick walls that used to be storerooms for miso are nice and cool in summer. The corridor, dark even during the day, with little rooms opening off it, reminds me of a prison.

A pool of fluorescent light leaks from the door of the toilet at the end of the hall. Step, step, step . . . As we walk along the dark corridor, I feel like someone is watching us, but for some reason I cannot turn to look. The graveyards that I saw today must now stand in darkness, the wind blowing through them. Ghosts are probably flitting about the tombs, like nimble-footed creatures.

"Ever hear of the miso-licker?" Kawabe whispers.

"What?" Yamashita's voice shakes, expecting the worst.

"A ghost that licks miso. With a long tongue like a cat . . ."

"Cut it out!"

"Don't you get the feeling it might still be living here? That it might creep up from behind and lick your neck? *Slurp*!"

Yamashita catches his breath and freezes in his tracks. I glare at Kawabe and see his chalk-white face. He is shaking, too. Why does he have to go and tell a story like that when he is scared himself?

All three of us breathe a sigh of relief when we reach 139

the brightly lit room with its row of shining urinals. The sound of our wooden sandals echoes from the walls and ceiling. We line up in front of the urinals.

"You know, I'm afraid to go to the bathroom when I wake up in the middle of the night even when I'm in my own house. I try and hold it till I'm bursting, but there's no way you can sleep, right?" Yamashita says.

"I'm afraid, too," I confess, following Yamashita's example. "There's a sink by the toilet, and I really hate looking in the mirror over it."

The three of us finish at the same time, proof that we are true pals.

"You guys are dumb," Kawabe says to egg us on and keep us from going back out into the dark corridor. "If you're so afraid, don't go to the bathroom."

"But—"

"I just open the window by the bed."

"You pee out the window?"

"Yeah."

"But you live on the sixth floor!"

"No, stupid. It opens onto the veranda. There's a little moss growing there now."

Yamashita's face crinkles and he gives a short laugh. "I really hate the dark," he says seriously.

"Why?" Kawabe lowers his voice. "Why do you think people are afraid of the dark?"

"Hmmm . . . I don't know." Yamashita ponders the question. "It makes you feel like ghosts might be there . . ."

"Do you think it's a human instinct?" I say.

"Ah. Now think about that a little more deeply," Kawabe says eagerly.

"Oh geez," I groan. Kawabe is jiggling. He must

have gotten one of his flashes of inspiration. Honestly! As if he ever thinks deeply himself. Just look at the time. And the place! The fact that he demands we think a little more deeply right now is proof that he doesn't think.

"Because in the dark we don't know whether something is hiding there or not?" I venture, resigned to my fate.

"That's it!" Kawabe nods emphatically. "In other words, the unknown. That is the cause of fear."

"The cause of fear?"

"Take, for example—" Kawabe begins. He is wide-awake now, his eyes gleaming behind his glasses, which he doesn't even leave behind to go to the bathroom in the middle of the night. We stand in triangle formation, facing each other with our arms folded. In the old days people used to gossip around the well. And here we are gathered around the urinals.

"Take, for example, zombies, ghosts, and monsters. There are many different kinds, right? I have an encyclopedia of monsters and there are more than one hundred kinds in that book. And if you included monsters from other countries, there would be even more."

The concrete wall of the room sucks up Kawabe's whispering voice. Far away a clock strikes two.

"People thought up all those monsters and ghosts. People named them and drew pictures of them. That's proof that we really fear things which have no shape. If we decide what it looks like, give it a name, then we know what it is. And if we know what it is, we feel a little less afraid. Right?"

"So that story about the miso-licker was the same idea?"

"Yeah. It should help us feel less afraid." 141

"I wonder," Yamashita says, thinking even harder. "But I was scared."

"Maybe it's normal to be scared," I say. "Come on, let's go back."

We run down the dark corridor. If what Kawabe says is true, then he hasn't read enough of that encyclopedia.

The sky is very clear. Clouds float like islands drawn on a map, and a hawk seems to swim effortlessly through the atmosphere. Autumn has begun its descent to the earth.

There is a grove of trees on a plateau, and in the middle there is a playing field. It is really just a clearing, but there are two soccer goals. Even in this spot surrounded by trees, you can still hear the sound of the ocean.

In the morning we practice dribbling, lifting, and passing, and in the afternoon we divide into two teams for a scrimmage match. The sixth-graders on my team consist of me, Yamashita, Kawabe, and two others. The fourth- and fifth-graders have been broken up, too, so that the ages are evenly distributed between the two teams.

"Yamashita is goalie. Okay?"

"Again?" Yamashita complains. He is a slow runner, so he always winds up as the goalkeeper. "I can't stand the pressure."

"Quit complaining. We won't let the ball past the defense," Kawabe says, and Yamashita shuts up.

I don't want to lose to Sugita and Matsushita's team either, so I give him a thump on the shoulders and say, "We're counting on you." But he looks at me with reproach.

"But you're perfect for goalkeeping," I say lamely.

"Because I'm fat, right?" is his parting shot as he waddles off to stand in front of the goal.

"Give it all you've got, guys!" Sugita yells. Show-off. I think about giving my own team an encouraging yell, but the whistle blows while I'm trying to think of something to say, and the match begins.

If nothing else, Kawabe is fast. He zips past his opponents like lightning. He roars ahead of Sugita, who is trying to intercept him, passes the ball to me, and I shoot it in past Matsushita, their goalkeeper, before he can even move. It is an exquisite play.

"Don't just stand there!" Sugita roars as if he were the coach. Roar all you like, Sugita, I think. He always does that. Whenever we have a match he acts as if he is the most important member of the team.

Sugita isn't as swift as Kawabe, but he is fast enough. It is his footwork, though, that is really impressive. He can lift the ball over a hundred times easily. I am lucky if I can get to twenty. When he really starts moving, the ball follows him around like a pet dog and won't be separated from him.

For Sugita, his team just gives him an opportunity to show off. He hogs the ball and slips past our defense to score three consecutive goals. Then he kicks the ball right between my legs, claims it once again, and scores. Darn! Of course, Yamashita is so nervous he freezes in place, with only his eyes moving back and forth. "Yamashita! Move!" the coach yells, and Yamashita fidgets nervously in front of the goal, looking like he is about to cry.

Whenever he scores a goal, Sugita raises his chin a little and flips his hair back as if to say, "Hmph. Piece of cake." And whenever Kawabe sees him show off like that, he starts his usual jiggling.

"Your pants are going to fall down," I warn Kawabe, and in answer he leaps into the air shrieking, "*Kiyeh!*," slicing the air with his hands and feet in mock karate chops. A fifth-grader who is bigger than Kawabe sees him and snickers. If he is going to yell, he should have picked something more appropriate, like "Let's get 'em!" or "Let's go!" or "Fight!" but when I try to think of something to yell myself, I can't, so I just shake my head in disgust.

Our team's desperate battle continues. A fourth-grader falls and starts crying, and none of our shots score. Sugita is charging toward our goal. As center back I go out to intercept him. Kawabe follows tenaciously after, as though stuck to him.

Just then I notice a fifth-grader on Sugita's team off to one side nearer the goal. He is waving his arms at Sugita, who is farther from the goal than he is. Then everything happens at once. I shout "Mark him!" to our right back, a fourth-grader who is idly picking his nose, 145 while the coach yells, "Sugita, pass!" and at the same instant I feel the ball whiz by me on the left. It is a very long shot. Sugita ignored the fifth-grader. I look behind me thinking, We're done for! and see Yamashita standing grimly in front of the goal. His eyes are opened wide like a cat caught in the glare of a car's headlights. What happens next occurs in a single instant, yet I see it as clearly as if it were a video going in slow motion. The ball revolves slowly toward the goal. Fear crosses Yamashita's face; then he freezes, presses his lips together, and shuts his eyes tightly.

The coach roars, "Move! No! No, don't move! Grab the baaaaall!!!" The next moment the ball stops dead. As though stuck to Yamashita's face. Then it falls to the ground and bounces several times, coming to rest at Kawabe's feet. For an instant no one moves. We stand still as stone staring in amazement at Yamashita's bright-red face.

"Nice play, Yamashita!" Kawabe yells, and gives the ball a good kick.

"You guys sure make a perfect trio, don't you?" Sugita jeers. It is suppertime and he is sitting on the other side of the table in the large tatami dining room. He must have been furious that his team lost. After Yamashita took the ball in the face, our team excelled themselves and turned the tide to win the game.

"You can't even go to the bathroom by yourselves. You just have to stick together, don't you?" Sugita sneers. "Hey, everybody, these three are so afraid of ghosts they go to the bathroom together."

"Three together, pee together. The pee-pee trio,"

Matsushita jeers, as though he has been waiting for this chance. "Mommy! Come! I need to pee."

Yamashita bristles. He still has cotton stuffed up his nose because it bled after the ball hit him in the face.

Even the fourth- and fifth-graders must have heard Sugita and Matsushita. The coach, who is sitting at the table next to ours, guffaws loudly. I feel betrayed. Grownups can be pretty insensitive, I have found.

"Ghosts? Ha! You think we're afraid?" Kawabe retorts.

"Liar!" Sugita accuses. I remember then that his room is near the toilets. He must have seen us the night before.

"Well, aren't you afraid of them?" Kawabe demands in a threatening voice. Not even that stops them from sniggering.

"Not at all," Sugita answers, looking perfectly cool. He really is a pain. "I don't believe in ghosts."

"What are you going to do if they really do exist?"

"Aren't you a little baby," Sugita says, looking into Kawabe's face with amusement. "Why don't you go back to kindergarten?"

Matsushita laughs as if he thinks this hilarious.

"How do you know if they exist or not?"

"Let me tell you," Sugita begins, saying each word slowly and carefully as though explaining to a little child. "When you die, that is the end. That is why there can be no ghosts. Spirits, heaven, hell—these are just ideas made up by weak and cowardly people. People who are failures at life make up these things to comfort themselves. That's what my father says." I want to punch his thin-skinned hooked nose off his face.

147

"Would you like some more soup?" A bent old woman carries a large pot. It is the coach's grandmother.

"Oh yes, please," Yamashita says, holding out his bowl as though to escape Sugita's taunting. The old woman pours him a bowlful of miso soup with whitefish.

I wonder how old the coach's grandmother is. Eighty? Ninety? Maybe even older. I can't tell. Her back is so bent it is taller than her head, so that she does not seem to be a member of the human race. One thing's for sure, she is definitely the oldest person I have ever met.

I met her last year and the year before that, but I had just thought of her as old and nothing else. Now, however, I realize that I am wrong, for the coach's grandmother is not at all like the old man we visit so often. For one thing, she is much older, and for another, perhaps because she lives so near the sea, her skin is tanned very dark, with deep, hard creases. Her mouth is like a crack wreathed in wrinkles, so that you wonder where her lips have gone, but her teeth seem strong and healthy, and unlike the old man, she isn't missing any. She has a large mole on her left cheek. I seem to notice these details now.

"This soup is delicious," Yamashita says, putting the bowl to his lips as soon as she has filled it.

"That's because you worked up such a sweat today," she says. She holds out her hand toward me. Her fingers are slightly crooked, as though they are stiff. I put my bowl gently in her hand.

"It must be the miso that makes it taste so good," Yamashita says. He nods to himself with his nose still stuck in his bowl.

"Do you make this miso here?" I ask.

"No, not anymore. Even if we wanted to, it would be impossible."

"Why?"

She puts the bowl of soup down carefully in front of me and says, "Well, you see . . ." She settles herself down to talk, but then seems to change her mind. "No, it's better not to talk about it."

"Oh come on, please? Tell us," Kawabe urges, as though sensing some kind of secret. We look at the old woman expectantly. She is an expert at telling horror stories. Every year she tells us stories of things that have happened on this island. And it gives me a thrill to think that, this year, the story is set in this very house.

"You mustn't tell anyone else, though. You understand?" She stares at each one of us with her large eyes. Yamashita and Kawabe and I, and even Sugita and Matsushita, lay down our chopsticks and lean forward. The kids at the other table probably can't hear her.

"Well, of all the places in this area making miso, this house was the best and the richest. So why did they stop? This is what my older sister told me. My sister who died young." Here she pauses. If she does it to rivet our attention, it is very effective.

"You see, a woman died here."

Kawabe gasps. Yamashita puts his hand to his mouth just like a girl. Sugita looks at Matsushita as if to say, "I knew it." And Matsushita responds with a weak laugh.

"It was several generations ago. The master of the household was a rake. He had married into the family, and at first he worked very hard. But little by little he lapsed into sloth and began idling about. The woman who died, well, she had been divorced by a nearby moneylender, and how it came to pass I don't know, but the master of this house and that woman . . ." The old woman presses her wrinkled lips together firmly.

"Had an affair!" Sugita yelps.

She frowns at Sugita reprovingly and nods. "He had the woman sneak in through the back door so they could meet secretly in one of the miso storerooms."

Despite the noise of the others eating dinner, the woman's soft voice penetrates clearly.

"One day he heard someone looking for him outside the storeroom. He told the woman he would come back for her and left her there alone, barring the door securely. It was his wife who had been looking for him. A barrel of miso had to be delivered to the other side of the mountain, but the deliveryman had come down with the measles. She asked her husband to go instead. The man had no choice. He climbed up onto the cart with its load of miso and set out. What happened next, nobody knows, but the man drove off the cliff, cart and all, and died on the rocks below."

Kawabe gives a little laugh. "That's what you get for cheating on your wife."

The old woman nods slowly, her eyes closed. She looks like a great big wise old frog.

"When they retrieved his body, they found that his belly had been split open like a pomegranate. A terrible way to die. The key to the storeroom was given to his wife. Whether or not she knew that the other woman was there, I don't know, but she did not lift a finger to open the storeroom door. For days and days, the sound of fingernails scraping on the other side of the thick wooden door could be heard. Then finally the noise ceased.

"That was when they stopped making miso. The wife made this place into an inn because of the rumors that the divorced woman had died here. Guests at the inn would come from far away, so they couldn't possibly know about the rumors."

The old woman laughs with her mouth closed, as if looking to us for agreement. The vertical lines around her mouth lengthen while her eyes are hidden by deep wrinkles. It is as if someone you thought you knew suddenly removed a mask from their face. It gives me the shivers.

"The work was all done by a single carpenter, but the carpenter dropped dead as soon as he was finished. Before he died, in his delirium, he said that he had found a dead woman, completely naked, in the storeroom . . . She had shoved her head into a vat of miso and suffocated. The poor thing. She must have gone mad toward the end. The woman's face had been pickled by the miso and was untouched by rot.

"But to this day we can't keep any extra miso in this house. It goes bad and starts to smell like face powder. Her anger at her fate cursed the miso and there's nothing we can do but accept it."

We sit in silence. The white strips of fish in our soup look like the woman's skin covered in white powder.

"The strangest thing, however"—she hunches over even more, stretches out her wrinkled neck like a turtle, and sticks out her chin, as if she has much, much more to tell us. Her big eyes move back and forth—"was that my older sister said she heard a sound like the grating of fingernails coming from one of the miso storerooms."

"But—that was a long time ago, wasn't it?" I ask. I try to say it nonchalantly, but my voice is a high-pitched squeak.

"Yes, it was a long, long time ago. But she did say that she heard it. And that she could never forget it. And I can't help thinking that that is the reason she died so young. It must be." She closes her eyes and nods again to herself.

"About that storeroom," Sugita asks nervously. "Which room is it?"

"Well, you know, I was just a little girl when I heard this story from my sister. But—"

"But?"

"Just recently, one of the guests staying at this inn, in the middle of the night—"

"In the middle of the night . . . ?"

"They heard something go *scritch-scratch* . . ."

"Tell us which room!" Sugita wails.

"Mother! Stop that talk now," the coach's father says from behind me in a displeased tone of voice. I just about leap out of my skin.

"She's lying. Making it up. It's her hobby, or perhaps I should say bad habit, making up stories like that. You know that."

"Yeah, sure. Sure. Ha, ha, ha," Sugita says, trying to force a laugh but not succeeding very well. Kawabe is jiggling as usual, and Yamashita is staring into his soup bowl as though it has swallowed up his soul. Matsushita's mouth is hanging half open.

The old woman rises, grasps the soup pot, and starts to walk away.

"It wasn't true, was it?" I ask, but the old woman just laughs.

"She's a crazy old lady, that one. She'll be punished for this someday, that's for sure." The coach's father is laughing, too. But Kawabe, Yamashita, and I, and Sugita and Matsushita as well, don't touch our soup after that.

That night the three of us go to the bathroom together again. We are defiant. After all, when you're scared, you're scared.

But when we get there, we see that someone has gotten there first. Sugita and Matsushita. Their backs are turned to us and they are in the middle of their business. A pee-pee duo. Not only that, but they have brought along two fifth-graders who were obviously shaken awake and forced to come without understanding why. They are practically asleep on their feet, their sleep-swollen faces lit by the bright fluorescent light. This is certainly worse than our trio. It is a toilet quartet.

I scrape my fingernails on the glass of the door to the toilets. *Screech-screech*. The sight of Sugita and Matsushita at that moment is priceless. They both leap about three feet straight up in the air, still peeing. As a result, they both wet their pants. I feel great.

"Hey there now. Don't pee your pants," Kawabe jeers.

In the next instant Sugita leaps on Kawabe. It is so sudden that Kawabe is pushed down on the floor, and before he has time to fight back, Sugita snatches his glasses.

"That's not fair!" I yell, grabbing Sugita's arm as he tries to smash the glasses on the floor. Sugita lets go of 153 the glasses and grabs my hair. I punch the side of his face as hard as I can. He yanks my hair with all his might. I can feel my head growing hotter. What follows is a real mess. We roll across the floor still locked together, kicking, punching, and biting. It is as if something that has been holding me back until now is suddenly gone. My body is wide-awake, my head is clear, and I feel an unbelievable strength well up inside me. If Sugita hadn't gone for Kawabe's glasses, I probably wouldn't have gotten so angry. The only thing I know is a feeling that a door has opened inside me with a loud click. And the memory in a corner of my mind of the time I had stopped Kawabe from attacking Sugita. The time when Sugita had made fun of Kawabe's father . . . I cannot stand to feel guilty again like I did then.

"What the hell do you think you're doing?!" Though we hear the coach bellowing at us, Sugita and I do not stop. I am startled by the surprisingly satisfying sound of a loud smack. I have slapped the coach in the face.

When we are finally separated, I notice that all the lights are on in the corridor. The coach raps Yamashita and Matsushita on the head with his knuckles where they stand, still struggling, each with the collar of the other's pajamas grasped in his fist. Then he throws Kawabe's glasses to Kawabe, who is crawling about the floor looking for them. The two fifth-graders still stand like thick-headed zombies.

Sugita's nose is bleeding. His pajamas are a mess. Serves him right, I think, and then notice that all the buttons have been torn off mine.

The coach has steam coming out his ears. "And just
what time do you think it is!?"

Bong! the wall clock answers. One lazy bong as if it has a screw loose. The curious crowd of spectators poking their heads out of their rooms snorts with laughter.

"The rest of you, get back to bed!" And their heads whip out of sight.

My lip burns and throbs. When I touch it, it doesn't feel like my own lip.

"Kiyama!" The coach glares at me. I am so mad, I glare right back. "What a face! Go look in the mirror."

I stand up unsteadily and look in the mirror. I really do look awful. My lip is swollen like a piece of cod roe.

We go to the coach's room, where he pours disinfectant on our wounds. It stings like fire. Matsushita makes such a fuss when a little is put on his arm that the coach raps him one more time with his knuckles. I bear it by gritting my teeth and glaring at Sugita. Sugita has cotton stuffed up his nose and, as is to be expected, is glaring at me.

"Looks like you didn't get enough exercise this afternoon. If you're feeling that energetic, you may as well clean the toilets. You hear me?"

"What?!" Yamashita, Kawabe, and Matsushita cry in unison.

"But Kiyama started it!" Sugita protests just as I yell, "Sugita, you dirty creep!"

"Quiet!" Lightning has struck. We all stand in shock. "You can clean the bathtub too. And no sleep until it is spotless. Spotless, do you understand?"

I stand up without another word. At such times, he who accepts defeat gracefully wins.

14

"Look at this! Over here!" Yamashita shouts excitedly, hunching over the ground. It is a bud. We have been gone only four days but our cosmos have definitely grown.

"Here's another one!"

Now and then a cool breeze blows, as though autumn has slipped down from the sky and is just waiting for the chance to show itself. Soon the entire yard will be covered with blooming flowers.

"Let's surprise him," Kawabe says, taking a stuffed toy frog from his cram-school bag. We bought it for the old man at the souvenir shop on the island. The distance between its eyes makes it look just like Kawabe without his glasses on, but Kawabe hasn't realized that. Yamashita and I burst out laughing when he kept looking at it in a puzzled way on the train back home, saying, "It's got a funny face, but for some reason I like it."

"Let's bet on what the old man's doing," Kawabe says.

"Taking a nap," Yamashita says promptly.

"Cleaning the bathtub," Kawabe says.

For some reason, nothing comes into my head. "I can't think of anything," I say.

"You have no imagination. Just make up any old thing."

"Um, okay. He's cutting his toenails."

We creep near the porch. The window is slightly open. Through the screen door we can see the old man lying on his futon. His hands are loosely clasped over his stomach on top of the thin summer quilt. We open the screen door quietly.

"I won," Yamashita whispers. But in the next instant we know. We feel it with a strange clarity deep inside ourselves. He is not asleep.

A sweet smell pervades the room. Grapes. Four bunches of grapes the color of the night sky lit up by a distant fire lie in a bowl by his pillow. He must have placed them there, thinking to eat them with us, and gone to sleep.

"Like a little kid getting ready for a picnic," Yamashita says, wiping his teary eyes on the sleeve of his T-shirt. Kawabe is crouched in the corner with his back turned. Occasionally I can hear stifled sobs.

Silently I pick up one grape and slowly peel it. The small juicy fruit quivers in the palm of my hand.

157

"Here, eat." I hold the grape out to the old man. "Come on, eat. Please?"

I have read of people who in death look like they are sleeping. But the old man does not look like that. I don't mean that he is not at peace. In fact, he is even smiling a little, as though very content. But he is not asleep. He is dead. What is left is only his body, not the old man himself. That's how I feel. He will never again take up this body and talk with me or eat with me. His face has shrunken a little, and the shiny pate of his balding head seems like a patch of parched earth where the plants have all shriveled up and died.

It is the first time I have ever seen a dead man, but I do not feel frightened in the least. At that moment, all the ghosts and monsters which so terrified and fascinated us slip far from my mind. The old man's body lies there, gentle and familiar, like an old pair of worn clothes.

There is so much I want to tell him. About the practice match, about sleeping in a miso storeroom, about the horror story the old woman told us, about the first big fight I have ever had in my life, about cleaning the toilets until dawn, about the graveyards on the island, about the sea glittering like the back of a fish, about how I could hear the sounds within my own body when I dove into the ocean . . . So many things to tell, questions to ask. Images of how the old man would respond crowd before my eyes. Yet I wasn't even able to remember what he looked like until just a short time ago. When we were at soccer camp, I had talked with the old man in my mind every night before going to sleep, telling him all about what had happened during the day.

As if practicing for when I returned home. I enjoyed it very much. Pulling the covers over my head so the others wouldn't see, I had laughed, ranted, boasted, and even almost cried as I fell asleep.

I press the grape against his lips. Expecting its juice to somehow loosen his closed mouth. Say something. Anything. Just say something. If you will just speak to me, I will be your slave for the rest of my life. I'll weed your garden. Massage you. Take the garbage out. Do the laundry. I'll even feed you sashimi every day. So please, please, don't go yet . . .

But he cannot hear me. And I finally begin to cry.

Someone from the Welfare Office brings a medical examiner, and then everything begins to happen very quickly. Suddenly the old man's house is invaded by grownups. As for us, we only answer a few questions that a policeman asks us. "What time did you come here? Did you have some reason for coming? What relation are you to this man? Why did you come?"

"We came because we wanted to!" Kawabe yells, and that is the end of the questions.

We stay by the old man's side despite the looks of the neighborhood women. When it gets dark, Yamashita's mother and mine come to take the three of us home. I don't want to go. But I have no strength left in my body to even say, "I don't want to go."

That night I can't sleep. I keep remembering things and stare out the window of my room. I can't see the old man's house. There are too many buildings and apartments in the way. I wonder if the light is on. Is someone there? I close my eyes. In his darkened room, 159 only the television is on. In its flickering blue light, I feel that I can see the old man's back as he stands there all alone washing the grapes. "I'm here," I whisper in a small voice. And I feel something soft filling just a little the gaping hole in my heart. I whisper many times, "I'm here."

I can hear the distant sound of fireworks. In the darkness of the sky, the sound of invisible fireworks. One . . . two . . . three . . . And before I know it, I have fallen asleep.

The next day the screen doors have been taken off the old man's house and the glass doors are opened wide. Inside is a small altar, white chrysanthemums, and a coffin which somehow seems strangely large in that room . . .

The son of the old man's older brother had traveled from the country and is sitting on the porch with members of the neighborhood association. Neighborhood women are gathered in groups of threes and fours in the garden, talking in low voices. They all hold fans or handkerchiefs, as if their black mourning clothes are too hot for comfort. They swat at the mosquitoes buzzing about their ankles and trample the cosmos. The priest finally arrives thirty minutes late, completing his prayers swiftly and offering incense. Then the coffin is opened. The old man is unbelievably shrunken and stiff. I don't want to look, I think. This isn't him. Kawabe and Yamashita begin to cry. I begin to cry, too. But at the same time I feel another me, separate from the person who is crying, asleep inside me, as if everything were covered by an indistinct veil.

We are driven in a stranger's car to the crematorium, where the big steel doors open as though they have been waiting to swallow the old man. Swiftly and smoothly, on rails.

"It hardly makes any smoke."

"Mmm."

Sitting on a bench gazing at the chimney of the crematorium, I suddenly notice what a hot day it is. It is really hot. As if summer, which has already left, had been called back one last time.

"I'm glad we bought the frog," Kawabe says. He had placed the stuffed toy we bought at the souvenir shop inside the coffin.

"Hey, you kids." The son of the old man's older brother approaches us, loosening his necktie. "I want to ask you something." Having crowded us over to one side of the bench, he sits down. "It's about my uncle."

It takes me a couple of seconds to realize that he means the old man. He doesn't look like the old man at all, although he is his nephew, and he doesn't look either sad or happy that the old man has died.

"My uncle, he left money to some woman."

We look at each other. It must be Yayoi Koko.

"Honestly. I had no idea he had saved so much," he says, wiping the sweat off the bridge of his nose. His handkerchief is a vulgar check pattern. He could at least have brought a white one on such an occasion as this. "And he wrote that I should ask you where she lives."

"You mean there was a letter?" Kawabe asks in surprise.

"Yeah," he replies grumpily. "He wrote that if he died someone should be sure to contact one of you."

We are stunned.

"It's all my fault!" Kawabe snuffles. "I was the one who wanted to see a dead person in the first place . . ."

"Don't cry," I say, looking up at the chimney. That's what the old man would say if he were here. Don't cry. But Kawabe just cries even harder.

"He wrote down all three of your names, but I didn't believe it was you at first. I mean, after all, it seemed impossible . . ."

"You didn't think that he could mean a bunch of kids," I say, and the man looks back at me.

"Well, yeah, that's right." He stands up as though flustered. "I guess he had no one else. He always did whatever he felt like," he says, and then leaves.

The white smoke drifting from the tip of the chimney melts into the blue sky. I open my eyes very wide and stare at the smoke. Blown by the wind, it seems to sway happily. I have to keep watch. Until the very end, without taking my eyes off it.

The bits of bone in the old man's ashes are pure white. Some are flat, others are curved, and still others are like the fossils of shells. We have to use chopsticks to pick up the bones, passing them from one set of chopsticks to the other, then placing them in an urn. Kawabe and I gingerly pick up one shaped like the center of an orchid. "That bone is from the throat," the undertaker remarks. "You're very lucky it has retained its shape so well." All three of us listen attentively. The old man has gone somewhere far beyond our reach. Looking at his bones, I realize for the first time that some part of me has been hoping that just maybe the old man might come back to life again. But now I know that that can never be, and in my heart I feel strangely peaceful and clear.

If the old man had lived longer, I would have talked with him about many things and he would have advised me. I am worried about my exams, and I have no idea what I want to be when I grow up. He would have listened to my problems. Next summer, we might have eaten watermelon together again and he might have treated us to more fireworks. And when I grew up, we might even have drunk beer together at the oko-nomiyaki restaurant. Now we never will. It makes me feel terribly lonely. Terribly alone. But in the end, that is my problem. The old man, he lived a good enough life. His white bones tell me that. That he lived his very best. In my heart I tell him, "I'll do my best, too."

There is a dry sound as the lid is put on the urn. Our summer holidays are over.

15

"We're skipping cram school today. Got that?" Kawabe says during lunch hour. It is the first Thursday in October. "They're finally going to start today."

Yamashita and I nod silently.

After school we gather at the old man's house. Cosmos bloom across the entire yard. The stems are short and the flowers small, but they look like little flames burning amid the weeds.

"What's going to happen to this place?" Yamashita is gently stroking the closed storm doors. "They'll build an apartment complex or something here, maybe."

The front door is locked. The knob is rough with sandy dirt. Kawabe is wandering off toward the garden when he suddenly hunches down and begins jiggling.

Tomorrow the house is to be torn down. Although it has been empty for only a month, it already seems very dilapidated. The green storm doors and the beige wooden walls look dull. I notice that the clothesline has disappeared. Perhaps it was already gone on the day of the funeral . . .

We silently gather the cosmos flowers and leave the garden. As he passes the front door, Yamashita looks back and stares down at the broken stone step. The same step he had put the sashimi on.

"Let's go!" Kawabe says, and strides off with his face buried in his bouquet of flowers.

"I'm worried," Yamashita says. "I'm worried that we'll forget this house."

I am, too. At home in my room I tried to remember the old man. But the harder I tried, the more I felt all my memories slipping away from me, and I couldn't stand it.

"So I'm going to memorize this stone, for sure. I'm not very smart, but I think I can at least remember this one thing."

I close my eyes so tightly that tears almost come out. Lights flash behind my lids. Then I open them again suddenly. And for one second I see the front door open and the old man's head peering out. I even hear the sound of the door opening.

"I'm going to put these flowers in my room," I say. I turn my back on the locked door and start to walk away.

"Me, too. I'll keep them on my desk."

"Then we can study harder."

"Yeah, you're right. We'd better."

I have been putting off my studies until now, but I no longer feel like avoiding them. I begin to devour practice tests like a hungry animal every day. It is almost time for exams.

My mother is hospitalized about the time the cosmos on my desk start to wilt. It is her liver, maybe because she drinks too much. When my father first heard that she was ill, he was angry. He cursed her, called her "Stupid!" as if he couldn't suppress his annoyance. My mother cried and said, "I'm sorry. I'm sorry." But now that she has been in the hospital for a while, my father is beginning to leave work early and visit her on his way home. Before he had only thought of work, work, work. I get home late because of cram school, but somehow the two of us manage to survive without my mother. Most of the time we make do with store-bought dinners, but sometimes I make simple things, using my mother's cookbooks. Grilled fish, salad, even an omelet, which fell to pieces. My father eats them all, saying they are delicious. I will never forget the time my father made stew. He spent half the day simmering vegetables and meat, and when it was done, we took it pot and all to the hospital and ate it with my mother. As she ate, she began to cry, and I must admit that I felt rather exasperated. But my father urged her to eat so gently that my own throat felt all tight and funny.

On the way home, my father asked me, "What are you going to do when you grow up?"

I was astonished. It was the first time he had ever asked me something like that since I was very small.

"I don't know," I said, and thought a little. "It may not be a job, but I think I'd like to write."

"A writer, huh?" It was my father's turn to be surprised. "A novelist?"

"I don't know if I could ever be a novelist," I said, my ears getting hot. "But I want to write things down. I think it would be great to write down the things that I don't want to forget and share them with other people."

My father listened silently.

"There are so many things that I don't want to forget. Someday I bet I'll even write about today." And about this summer, I added to myself.

"That's not a bad idea." My father slowly raised his face to gaze up at the sky. Orion was shining. Winter had already come to the sky.

Studying hard since fall has been worth it. I got into a private junior high school. My dad was really happy and bought me a notebook bound in leather and a foreign-made fountain pen. A card with the words *To the future writer* written on it was inside the notebook. This is too much, I thought, and decided that I wouldn't tell him that I had really wanted a word processor.

I used the notebook to work on a short story called "Y-kun's Story." I didn't manage to finish it in time for our graduation collection, but I rewrote it and read it at our class farewell party, to which everyone brought something to share. I was so nervous the night before that I couldn't sleep, but it went very well. The class roared with laughter. The teacher even asked me to recite it at the student-teacher graduation dinner. It felt so good, maybe the best feeling I have ever had in my life. Yamashita, upon whom the story was based, however, was not very pleased, remarking that it was really just a story about a fat guy who gets dumped by a girl.

Yamashita, unfortunately, didn't pass his exams.

"Oh well," he says. "Maybe now my mother will give up and let me run a fish shop." Yamashita is still fat, but he is growing taller and seems even more like a fish-store owner. Kawabe and I are impressed, and maybe a little envious, that he already knows what he wants to be when he grows up.

Kawabe didn't sit for the exams. His mother is going to remarry, and because of her new husband's job, they will be moving far away, to Romania.

On graduation day the three of us walk home from school carrying our diplomas.

"Too bad, Kiyama," Yamashita says. "Just when Tajima was starting to like you."

Tajima and Sakai will be going to the same public junior high as Yamashita. I am a little envious.

The only thing to look forward to at junior high is being able to wear long pants. I am still tall and stringy, and I am hoping that long pants might look better on me.

"But then there'll probably be someone at your new school," Yamashita adds as I remain silent.

"Probably people like Sugita and Matsushita, too," I say. The faces of all the kids I have met in the last six years run through my mind.

"I wonder what Romania is like." Yamashita walks along banging his knees rhythmically with his diploma case.

We come to a halt. It is the place where the old man's house had stood. The neighboring houses have all been torn down, too, and the whole area is now a parking lot.

"You know—" Kawabe says, staring at the ground, which is completely covered with asphalt. Our garden where we had planted the cosmos is now sleeping beneath it. "When my mom first told me she wanted to remarry, I said no. I had wanted a father so badly all that time, but when I thought of a stranger suddenly saying, 'I'm your father,' well . . . But that night I thought about it. I wondered what the old man would say if he were here."

"So that's why you agreed."

Kawabe nods. I know just how he feels. I often think about what the old man would say. And when I do, the answer comes to me much more easily than if I had pondered over it by myself. It's not living in the past. It feels much more sure and concrete.

"I'm going to do all right. We'll live together, the three of us, in a foreign country. We'll have to do all right, won't we?" Kawabe says, and nods in agreement with himself.

"You've really grown up," Yamashita says.

"You mean it?"

"Yeah, really."

I feel that if we stay here any longer my heart will burst. We walk on in silence and then at the corner say, "See you later," and part. We can't think of anything else to say. At the next crossing, I turn to the right, Kawabe turns to the left, and Yamashita keeps going straight. One step, two steps . . . I walk on slowly as though counting paces in a duel. But before I go ten steps Yamashita suddenly yells, "Hey! I forgot to tell you!"

He is still standing in the middle of the crossing. I 169

know I am looking at him eagerly. As if expecting something. Kawabe, who has retraced his steps, has that kind of look on his face, too. To part like this just doesn't seem right somehow.

Yamashita looks a bit disconcerted by our fixed gazes, but then he flashes us his biggest smile and says, "I can go to the bathroom by myself now. I'm not afraid anymore."

Kawabe and I are taken aback for an instant. Then Yamashita yells, "After all, we have a friend in the next world watching out for us! Doesn't that make you feel invincible?"

There is a short silence. Then Kawabe suddenly yells in his loudest voice, his eyes opened wide behind his glasses, "You bet!"

I nod frantically. And while I'm nodding I feel like jumping on top of Yamashita and giving him a great big bear hug. He says things so simply, but he's always right on target. How does he manage to do that?

Yamashita draws a deep, satisfied breath, turns his back on us, and runs off, saying, "See you!"

Kawabe and I stand stunned for a little while, staring after his receding figure. When I look at Kawabe, the kid who was always fidgeting nervously, he has on the sunniest expression I have ever seen. I feel a cool breeze blow through my heart, and then I say, "See you!"

"Yeah, see you again."

"Absolutely!" And I turn and run as fast as I can.